the cuban club

The Cuban Club

Roz met Tina at the Cuban
Brotherhood Club and Dance Hall
in Tampa, Florida, where ~~she was~~
~~Dina was a writer~~. Roz was spe-
one summer with his Uncle Buc
~~nig~~ construction ~~on~~ weekdays
~~to the weekends to be~~ ~~back~~ resting
and fishing on Sundays. Tina was ~~a~~ girlfriend
local girl, who went with her girlfriend to the a
~~crowd~~ at the Cuban club ~~on~~
nights.

Roy and his friend Ralp
fascinated big-eyed dusty the Cuban girl
come to Florida ~~how~~ with ~~r~~
on the first wave of emigre
fled ~~from Fidel Castro~~ the island following the revolution. T
~~wore makeup~~ bright red lips
hoop earrings and short skirts They danced u
~~did not spea~~

the
cuban club

STORIES

BARRY GIFFORD

Seven Stories Press
New York • Oakland • London

First trade paperback edition October 2018.

The following stories were written after the publication of the hardcover edition, and appear here for the first time in the paperback: "The Best Part of the Story," "Tell Him I'm Dangerous," "The Shadow Going Forward," and "Feeling the Heat."

Seven Stories Press
140 Watts Street
New York, NY 10013
sevenstories.com

Library of Congress Cataloging-in-Publication Data

Names: Gifford, Barry, 1946- author.
Title: The Cuban club / Barry Gifford.
Description: First edition. | New York : Seven Stories Press, 2017.
Identifiers: LCCN 2017004923 | ISBN 9781609807894 (hardcover); ISBN 9781609808600 (paperback); ISBN 9781609807900 (ebook)
Subjects: | BISAC: FICTION / Short Stories (single author). | FICTION / Literary. | LITERARY COLLECTIONS / American / General.
Classification: LCC PS3557.I283 A6 2017 | DDC 813/.54--dc23
LC record available at https://lccn.loc.gov/2017004923

Printed in the USA

9 8 7 6 5 4 3 2 1

ACKNOWLEDGMENTS

"Roy and the River Pirates" and "Lost Monkey" originally appeared in *Vice* magazine (New York). "The King of Vajra Dornei" appeared, in different form, in *The Up-Down* (New York, 2015). "A Long Day's Night in the Naked City (Take Two)" originally appeared, in different form, in *The 2nd Black Lizard Anthology of Crime Fiction* (Berkeley). "Mules in the Wilderness" appeared in *The Collagist* (Ann Arbor). "Dingoes" appeared in *Contrapasso* (Sydney). "The Colony of the Sun" appeared in the *Santa Monica Review* (Los Angeles). "The Religious Experience" and "The Cuban Club" appeared in *Narrative* (San Francisco). Several of these stories also appeared in *Confabulario*, the cultural supplement of *El Universal* (Mexico City). "The Best Part of the Story" originally appeared in the *Los Angeles Times*. "Tell Him I'm Dangerous" appeared in *Zoetrope All-Story* (San Francisco).

The following stories were published in *The Chicagoist* (Chicago). "Mona," "Mud," "King and Country," "Dark and Black and Strange," "Sick," "The Italian Hat," "I Also Deal in Fury," "Creeps," "Dingoes," "Chicago, Illinois, 1953," and "Role Model."

*This book is for
Phoebe and Asa*

"To die is nothing, it's only going from one room to another."
—Major-General James Hope Grant,
Incidents in the China War

"You may be witched by his sunlight . . . but there is the blackness of darkness beyond."
—Herman Melville, "Hawthorne and His Mosses"

"Shortly before his death, [a man] discovers that the patient labyrinth of lines traces the image of his own face."
—Jorge Luis Borges

AUTHOR'S NOTE

After publication of my collection *The Roy Stories* I had no intention of writing more about Roy. However, since he and his family and friends persisted appearing in my thoughts and dreams it seemed disloyal of me to ignore them. They're still talking and I'm still listening. I hope you'll keep reading.

—B.G.

CONTENTS

the cuban club

ROY AND THE RIVER PIRATES

Roy had no idea that this would be the last summer of his father's life. Roy was eleven years old and his father was forty-seven. His dad had always appeared strong and healthy. He smoked cigarettes and cigars and drank Irish whiskey but did not exhibit any obvious respiratory problems, nor did he ever give the slightest indication, in Roy's presence, of a lack of sobriety. The cancer that took Roy's father's life appeared in the fall and by the end of that winter he was dead.

His father and his father's second wife, Ellie, along with Roy's younger brother, Matthew, and older female cousin, Sally, were staying in a house his father was considering purchasing on Key Biscayne, Florida. Matthew was six and Sally, the younger daughter of Roy's father's sister, Talia, was almost fifteen. All of them lived in Chicago, although Roy, who lived mostly with his mother, frequently resided wherever she decided to spend time, alternating among Chicago, New Orleans and Havana. This summer of 1957, Roy's mother was with her current boyfriend, Johnny Salvavidas, in Santo Domingo, or travelling with him somewhere in the Caribbean. Roy did not expect to see her again until sometime in September.

Roy had a crush on Sally; he thought she was very pretty, with honey-blonde hair cut short, hazel eyes, unblemished skin and a slim figure. The best thing about her, though, was how naturally kind she was, even-tempered with a good sense of humor, and not at all stuck up. Sally was a straight talker, too, and she could be silly in a good way; she kidded around easily with both Roy and Matthew. Roy's father said that Sally did not get along very well with her parents, and she had asked him if he would take her to Key Biscayne for the summer if it was all right with her mother and father. Talia told Roy's father that Sally was "different," that she had her own way of thinking and doing things, which too often conflicted with Talia and her husband Dominic's ideas of how Sally should behave. Roy's dad didn't know exactly what Talia meant but he and Ellie liked Sally so they agreed to take her with them to Florida.

"What do you think Talia and Dominic don't understand about Sally?" Roy's father asked his wife.

"She's too airy fairy for them," said Ellie. "Her parents are all about business. If it's not about money, it's not worth their time. Sally's not like that."

Roy liked looking at his cousin. Sally was the first girl he knew who made him feel a little goofy just by looking at her. Whenever Sally noticed Roy staring, she smiled at him and sometimes brushed the hair off of his forehead with her hand.

The river pirates struck on the third night. Roy, Matthew and Sally had draped their bathing suits to dry over the back fence after they were finished swimming late that afternoon and left them there overnight. When they came out to get them the next morning, the bathing suits were gone. The intracoastal canal flowed right behind the house, making it easy for anyone on a boat to steal items of clothing hung over the back fence.

"We have to find out who took our bathing suits," Roy told Sally and Matthew. "It had to be river pirates."

"This is a canal," said Sally, "not a river."

"You mean real pirates?" asked Matthew. "With swords and patches over one eye and a black flag with a skull and crossbones on it?"

"Probably just kids in a rowboat who live around here," said Sally.

"We'll find out," Roy said. "Come on."

"Come on where?" Sally asked.

"Talk to the neighbors. Somebody might have an idea about who the thieves are."

None of the residents on the block had any suggestions about who could be responsible for the thefts, so Roy, Sally and Matthew decided to camp out at night in the yard and surprise the pirates if and when they came by again. As before, they hung their new bathing suits over the back fence after they had ended swimming for the day, and as soon as it was dark outside prepared their bedding on the grass. Ellie and Roy and Matthew's father both agreed that it was a good plan but asked what the kids intended to do if the thieves returned.

"Shoot 'em!" said Matthew. "I've got my bow and arrow set."

"The arrows have rubber tips," said Sally.

"We can describe 'em and get the name of their boat and track them down," Roy added.

"We'll give the information to the cops," Matthew said.

"No cops," said his father. "Handle it yourselves."

Roy and Sally and Mathew camped out in the yard several nights in a row but the river pirates did not appear. Of the three, Matthew was the most obviously disappointed. Roy was disappointed, too, but he enjoyed sleeping on the ground next to Sally. Early in the morning after what they decided would be their last night camping out, Mathew shot a few of his arrows over the fence into the canal.

"What did you do that for?" Roy asked him.

"I was pretending the pirates were there. They were probably afraid to come back."

Matthew walked over to the fence and shouted, "Chickens!"

For the remaining few weeks, Roy stole looks at Sally whenever he thought she wouldn't notice. She was always nice to him but this was not enough for Roy; he made up his mind that before they returned to Chicago he would try to kiss her.

Roy waited until the night before they had to leave, when Sally was alone in the yard standing by the back fence. He went out and stood next to her. His father and Ellie and Matthew were inside the house, packing.

"What are you doing out here?" Roy asked her.

"Oh, just looking at the water," she said. "I like seeing the reflection of the moon in it."

"It's too bad we never caught the pirates," said Roy,

Sally didn't seem so tall to him now; Roy figured he must have grown two or three inches since they'd been in Florida. He leaned over and kissed Sally on the corner of the right side of her mouth.

"What did you do that for?" she asked.

Sally was calm and smiled at Roy, as if she were not surprised.

"I like you a lot," he said.

"I like you a lot, too. I'm going to miss being down here with you and Matthew and your dad and Ellie."

"We'll see each other in Chicago."

"Sure, but it's not the same as Florida. The air is sweet and warm here, and the sky is always beautiful, especially at night."

"You're beautiful, too," said Roy.

Sally looked directly into his eyes. She was not smiling.

"Thank you, Roy," she said.

"I wish I were older," Roy said, "so I could be your boyfriend."

Sally looked back at the water, then up at the moon.

"There aren't any river pirates," she said. "Your father took the bathing suits and made me promise not to tell you and Matthew."

Roy didn't say anything. A large white bird flapped past them.

"You're not angry at me, are you?"

Roy walked back into the house.

"Come on, son," his father said, "give us a hand."

DINGOES

Roy liked to ride his bike up to Indian Boundary Park to look at the dingoes. There was a little outdoor zoo with a variety of smaller animals at the northern edge of the park, among them llamas, monkeys, ostriches and a patchy-furred, old brown bear. But it was the wild dogs of Australia that interested Roy the most. The dingoes were feisty, beige- or dun-colored knee-high canines that constantly fought among themselves and bared their fangs at the zoogoers who stared at them for more than a few seconds. Roy wondered why dogs were in a zoo, even supposedly wild ones. He guessed that in Australia dingoes ran in packs across a vast desert in the western part of the continent. He'd read about Australia in his fourth grade geography book which only mentioned dingoes in passing; most of the information about fauna in Australia was about kangaroos.

"Nasty little critters, aren't they?" a man said to Roy. "Now they're cooped up in this hoosegow."

Both Roy and the man were standing in front of the dingo enclosure on a cloudy day in August. Roy was nine years old and the man looked to Roy to be in his thirties or forties. Roy straddled his bicycle and watched and listened to the dingoes nip and yip at one another.

"The cage is too small for them," Roy said. "They need to be out running around in a desert."

The man was only slightly taller than Roy and thin with a gray-ish-brown mustache. He lit a cigarette then flicked the match through the bars at the dingoes.

"Wild dogs," the man said. "In China they'd be beaten to death. They've got police squads over there that do nothin' but run down stray dogs and club 'em over the head, then throw the bodies in a pile and burn 'em."

"These dogs are from Australia," said Roy. "They're not domesticated."

The man gave a little laugh with a hiccup in the middle of it. Roy had never heard anyone with a strange laugh like that before.

"Pretty fancy word you got there, kid. Domesticated. You learn that one in school?"

"Dingoes aren't meant to be pets," Roy said.

"Neither is that fat, scabby bear," said the man. "He shouldn't be in durance vile, either. These cages here are like cells in the Chateau d'If."

"What's that?" Roy asked.

"Prison island off the coast of Marseilles, in France. Like Alcatraz in San Francisco Bay. Nobody escapes from there."

"These animals can't escape from here, either. You seen the Chateau Deaf? Is it for deaf criminals?"

"Nope. It's d'If, not deaf. Name of the island is If. I read about it in *The Count of Monte Cristo*, a novel by Alexandre Dumas. Man named Edmond Dantes gets put away for life but after sixteen years digs a tunnel to the sea and swims away."

"I thought you said nobody escapes from there."

"Not in real life they don't. *The Count of Monte Cristo* is a story takes place in the nineteenth century. Edmond Dantes is an innocent man and after he gets out he finds a treasure a dying inmate at the Chateau d'If told him about and changes his name to Monte

Cristo before taking revenge on the three wrong customers who were responsible for having him take the fall for a crime he didn't commit."

The man dropped his butt then lit up another cig and again flicked his match at the dingoes.

"How come you're not in school, kid?"

"Summer vacation."

"I'm kind of on vacation, too."

Roy looked at the man again: his pale blue shirt had dark brown stains on it, as did his khaki trousers. When the man turned his head Roy saw that his left ear was missing; there was only a misshapen lump of skin where an ear should have been.

Roy climbed onto his bicycle seat and started to ride away but the man took hold of the handlebars with both of his hands.

"If you're clever," said the man, "you won't ever let anybody take advantage of you."

"What's that mean?"

"There are evil spirits haunt this earth who beguile good men and women and render them useless."

Not only was the man missing an ear but Roy noticed the mean-looking red and blue-black scar that ran almost the entire length of his hairline.

"I've got to go, mister. Let go of my bike."

The man released the handlebars, removed his cigarette from the right corner of his mouth and flicked it into the dingo cage.

As he was riding Roy remembered his grandfather telling him to listen carefully to what even crazy people said because the information might be useful later. When he got home Roy would ask him what in durance vile meant.

THE KING OF VAJRA DORNEI

One of Roy's most interesting childhood friends was Ignaz Rigó, who, following high school, had vanished into the greater world. Ignaz Rigó was a Gypsy kid whose family owned a two-story building on Pulaski Road next to the tuberculosis sanitarium. Roy had been to Ignaz's house a few times between the ages of thirteen and sixteen, and there never seemed to be fewer than twenty people, apparently all related, living there. The Rigó clan also occupied a storefront on Diversey, where the women, including Ignaz's mother and sisters, gave "psychic readings" and sold herbal remedies for a variety of complaints.

Ignaz, Senior, Roy's friend's father, called Popa, was always at the house on Pulaski whenever Roy went there. Regardless of the weather, Popa and an old man, Ignaz's maternal grandfather, named Grapellino, sat out on a second floor balcony on lawn chairs overlooking the street, talking and smoking. Both men were always wearing gray or brown Fedora hats, long-sleeved white shirts with gold cuff links buttoned at the neck, black trousers and brown sandals. Roy asked Ignaz what Popa's work was and Ignaz said that his father kept the family in order; and that Grapellino was a king in Vajra Dornei, which was in the old country. Roy asked Ignaz why, if his grandfather was a king in Vajra Dornei, he was living in Chicago. Ignaz told Roy that Lupo Bobino, a bad king from Moldova, had poisoned Grapellino's first wife, Queen

Nardis, and one of his daughters, and commanded a band of cut-throats that drove the Rigó clan out of Romania. Grapellino and Popa were planning to return soon to the old country to get their revenge and take back the kingdom stolen from them by Bobino's brigands.

"I'm goin' with them," Ignaz said. "We're gonna cut the throats of Lupo Bobino and everyone in his family, including the women and children. Last July, when I turned thirteen, Popa showed me the knife I'm gonna use. It once belonged to Suleiman the Magnificent, who ruled the Turks back when they kicked ass all over Asia. The handle's got precious jewels on it, rubies and emeralds, and the blade is made from the finest Spanish steel. Popa keeps it locked in a cabinet in his room. It's priceless."

Roy lost contact with Ignaz, who did not finish high school with him. Just before Christmas when Roy was twenty-one and back in Chicago on a visit from San Francisco, where he was then living, he went into the storefront on Diversey and asked one of Ignaz's older sisters, Arabella, who told fortunes and gave advice to women about how to please their husbands, where her brother was and what he was doing. Arabella, who was not married, had big brown eyes with dancing green flames in them, a hook nose, a mustache, and a thin, scraggly beard, as well as the largest hands Roy had ever seen on a woman. She told him that Ignaz was on a great journey, the destination of which she was forbidden to reveal. Arabella then offered Roy an herb called Night Tail she said would bring him good fortune with women, which he declined with thanks. Looking into Arabella's eyes, Roy remembered, made him feel weak, as did the thought of what she could do to him with her huge hands.

A year or so later, another former high school classmate of his, Enos Bidou, who worked for his father's house painting business in Calumet City, called Roy and told him that he'd run into Ignaz in East Chicacgo, Indiana, where Ignaz was repairing roofs and paving driveways with his uncle, Repozo Rigó.

"Remember him?" Enos Bidou asked. Roy did not, so Enos said, "He went to jail when we were still at St. Tim the Impostor. Got clipped for sellin' fake Congo crocodile heads and phony Chinese panda paws."

"When we were thirteen or fourteen, Ignaz told me he would go one day to Romania or Moldova with his father and grandfather Grapellino to take back Grapellino's lost kingdom."

"Well, I seen him a month ago in Indiana," Enos said. "He's got a beard now."

"So does his sister," said Roy.

REAL BANDITS

Roy was fourteen when he read a story about the Brazilian bandit Lampião in a book entitled *Famous Desperados*. Baseball practice had been called off because of rain, and he did not want to go home and have to listen to his mother complain about the shortcomings of her current husband, so Roy went to the neighborhood library and found the book lying by itself on a table. He sat down and looked at the contents page; there were chapters about Jesse James, the Dalton Gang, Baby Face Nelson, even Robin Hood, among others, all of whom he already knew something about, but Lampião—whose real name was Virgolino Ferreira da Silva—Roy had never heard of.

Lampião, it said in the book, means lantern, or lamp, in Portuguese. He lived and marauded with his gang in the 1920s and '30s in Northeastern Brazil, in the back country, or backlands, called the *sertão*. After his father was killed by police, when Virgolino was nineteen years old, he vowed to become a bandit and was given the nickname Lampião because he was the light that led the way for his followers, who included both men and woman. His girlfriend's name was Maria Bonita; she left her rancher husband to go with Lampião and ride with his band of outlaws, leaving her daughter, Expedita, to be raised by Lampião's brother, João.

The Brazilian word for bandits was *cangaceiros*, which came from the word *canga* or *cangalho*, meaning a yoke for oxen, because a *cangaceiro* carried his rifle over both of his shoulders like a yoke on an ox. Roy was enraptured by the place names of towns and backlands provinces that Lampião and his outfit traversed: Pernambuco, Paraíba, Alagoas, Chorrocho, Barro Vermelho, Campo Formoso, Santana do Ipanema, and many others. Lampião achieved a reputation similar to that of Robin Hood, sharing the spoils with the poor while robbing the rich. There was no real consistency about this, of course, as Lampião's generosities were often arbitrary, but nonetheless the myth grew over the years that he and his band, which varied in number between ten and thirty, moved freely about the backlands. He was regularly written about in newspapers and magazines throughout Brazil and dubbed the King of the *Cangaceiros*. A Syrian named Benjamin Abrahão even made a film starring Lampião and Maria Bonita.

Lampião and ten of his bandit gang, including Maria Bonita, came to an ignominious end, however, when they were gunned down by police in their hideout on the São Francisco River. The soldiers cut off hands and feet of the outlaws, to preserve as souvenirs, and each of the dead desperados was decapitated. Their heads were put on display first in Piranhas, and then in the local capital of Maceió. Finally, the heads of Lampião and Maria Bonita were sent to Salvador, the capital of Bahia, where they were exhibited in a museum. A photograph in the book of several of the heads, surrounded by their guns, hats and other belongings, fascinated Roy, especially since one of the faces closely resembled his own.

It was just drizzling when Roy came out of the library and there was very little light left in the sky, which was deep purple. As he walked toward his house, he thought about Lampião and his bandit brother, Ezekiel, nicknamed Ponta Fina, "Sureshot", escaping on horseback across the São Francisco, pursued by government soldiers, described by a witness as rawboned, dirty and desperately tired-looking. The bandits were constantly on the run, and in addition to their practice of thievery and murder, Lampião and some of his men occasionally castrated, branded or sliced off ears of those who opposed or offended them, believing that these particularly brutal acts of violence would intimidate others who would dare refuse to assist them or get in their way.

The rain began again, harder than before, so Roy stopped underneath the awning in front of Nelson's Meat Market on Ojibway Boulevard. The downpour reminded him of an episode described in the book of the time monsoon rains came suddenly one year near Raso da Catarina when Lampião and several of his cohorts were fleeing after raiding the property of a wealthy rancher. They were caught in open country and forced to take shelter under their standing horses and had to endure it when the horses urinated on him. Lampião was proud of the legend of himself as a rough, roguish, romantic character, glorified by journalists—some of whom he paid to propagate his myth—in the faraway big cities of Rio de Janeiro and São Paulo. Roy wondered if the dwarfish, skinny, half–blind bandit king had consoled himself with these thoughts as his bedraggled steed pissed on him.

A man and woman came and stood under the awning with Roy. The man was tall and thin and was wearing a brown suit with a red tie. The woman was wearing a green dress and her blonde hair was wet and matted from the rain. She fussed with it a little, then they both lit cigarettes. Roy noticed that the woman had a deep two–inch blue scar under her right eye she tried to conceal with make–up that had been mostly worn away by the rain.

"I heard they tied him to a tree," she said to the man, "then slit his throat and stole his wallet."

"No kiddin'," said the man.

"Yeah," she said, "took his shoes, too. They were real bandits."

HAITIAN FIGHT SONG (TAKE TWO)

Roy stood on the front steps of his school waiting for the car that was supposed to pick him up. An associate of his dad's, he'd been told, would be there at three o'clock to drive him to his father and his father's second wife Evie's house. Roy's mother, his father's first wife, from whom he'd been divorced since Roy was five, three years before, was out of town with her current boyfriend, Danielito Castro, so Roy was staying at his dad's until she came back to Chicago. His mother told Roy that Danielito Castro, whom Roy had briefly met once, wanted her to meet his family in Santo Domingo. She had been gone now for a week and had been uncertain about when she would return.

"I'll see how things go," his mother had said. "I don't think any of Danielito's family speaks English, other than Danielito, of course, so it probably won't be very long since I can't speak Spanish. You'll be fine with your dad and Evie, she's a nice girl. You won't even miss me."

Roy asked her where Santo Domingo was and she told him, "The Dominican Republic, it's on half of an island in the Caribbean Sea. The other half is a different country called Haiti. Danielito says the people there speak French. He told me the two countries are separated by a big forest and high mountains. He says the Haitians are very poor and are constantly trying to sneak into the DR, which is a richer country, so Dominican sol-

31

diers are permanently on guard along the border to keep them out."

"Probably a lot of the Haiti people hide in the forest until night when it's harder for the soldiers to see them and then sneak across," Roy said.

"Maybe, Roy. I'm sure I'll hear all about it when I'm there. Danielito says the Haitians are no good, that they don't like to work."

It was pouring when school let out. He did not have an umbrella or even a hood on his coat to pull up over his head so he hoped the person who was picking him up would not be late. Roy stood on the steps in the rain watching the other kids head for home or wherever they were going until he was the only one left. He waited for half an hour before he decided to walk to his father's house, which was more than two miles away. His own house, where he lived with his mother, was only a few blocks from the school, but nobody was there and he didn't have the key. He thought about going to one of his friends' houses but he knew that Evie was expecting him so he kept walking, hoping the rain would stop.

The rain did not stop. Other than for a few short intervals it continued in a steady downpour. On Ojibway Avenue, the main shopping street that led directly to his father and Evie's house, people hurried past him. Had he the fare, Roy would have taken a bus but he had not asked his dad for any money when he had dropped him off at school that morning. At the intersection of Ojibway and Western, in front of Wabansia's sporting goods store, where Roy had bought his first baseball glove, a Billy Cox model, a maroon Buick clipped a woman as she was stepping off the curb. She fell down in the street and the car's right rear tire ran over her black umbrella. The Buick turned the corner onto Western and kept going. The woman, who was wearing a red cloth coat, got up by herself. She bent down and picked up her umbrella, saw that it was broken and tossed it next to the curb. Roy was across the street from her when the accident happened. Nobody came to help her or ask her if she was all right and she walked across Ojibway and went into Hilda's Modern Dress Shop. Her right leg wobbled and Roy figured she'd been injured or the heel of her right shoe had broken off.

It took Roy a very long time to get to his dad and Evie's house and by the time he knocked on the front door the rain had weakened to a steady drizzle. When Evie opened the door and saw him looking like a drowned rat, she was horrified.

"Roy, what happened? Didn't Ernie Lento pick you up?"

"No, I walked. I didn't see anyone in a car at my school."

"You should have called me," said Evie. "I would have called a cab and come for you."

"I didn't have any money, or I would have taken a bus."

Evie took Roy in, helped him take off his wet clothes and wrapped two big towels around him.

"I'll make you some soup," she said, and headed for the kitchen.

Roy sat on the couch in the livingroom, covering his head with one of the towels. He looked around and for the first time noticed that there were no pictures on any of the walls, no paintings or photographs.

Evie came in and said, "The soup is heating up. I called your father and he said that Ernie Lento told him he was a few minutes late getting to the school but that you weren't where you were supposed to be."

"He must have been more than a little late," said Roy. "I waited on the front steps for around a half hour. Evie, how come you don't have any pictures on the walls in this room?"

"We have some framed photos on the dresser in our bedroom,"

she said. "Family photos. You've seen them. My parents and grandparents. Your grandparents, too, taken in the old country."

Evie left the room. Roy thought about Haitians creeping through a thick forest and waiting until night fell before hiking over a mountain range to get to the Dominican Republic. They probably didn't have umbrellas or any money on them, either. Danielito Castro had told Roy's mother that the Haitians didn't like to work but it had to be really hard work just to get from their side of the island to Santo Domingo or wherever they tried to get to in the Dominican Republic; and once they got there, if they survived beasts in the forest and bad weather in the mountains, the people spoke a different language.

Evie came into the livingroom carrying a bowl of tomato soup and a plate with Saltine crackers, a spoon and a napkin on it.

"Here's your soup, Roy. Blow on it because it's hot."

"Evie, what do you know about Haiti?"

"Why?" she asked. "Is that where your mother is?"

"No, she's in the Dominican Republic, another country that shares an island with Haiti. Are the people in Haiti really poor?"

"I think so, Roy. Most of them, anyway, certainly not all of them. There's always a ruling class who have more of everything. The only thing I know about Haiti is that it's the only country that was taken over by people who once were slaves. They had to fight for their freedom."

"My mother's friend Danielito Castro says the Haitians are no good and don't like to work."

"I'll tell you who's no good," Evie said. "I'll bet that crumb bum Ernie Lento stopped in a bar and was drinking with his race-track buddies. That's why he wasn't at your school on time, if he even got there. Your dad will find out. Eat your soup."

34

THE CUBAN CLUB

Roy met Tina at the Cuban Brotherhood Club and Dance Hall in Tampa, Florida, when he was fourteen. Roy was spending the summer with his uncle Buck working construction on weekdays, resting on Saturdays and fishing on Sundays. Tina was a local girl who went with her girlfriends to the dances at the Cuban Club on Saturday nights.

Roy and his friend Ralph were fascinated by the big-eyed, dusky Cuban girls who had come to Florida with their families in the first wave of emigrés who fled the island following the revolution. These girls wore make-up, bright red lipstick, large gold hoop earrings and short skirts. They danced only with one another and did not speak to white boys. Mostly they sat together in folding chairs in a corner of the dance hall and never stopped chattering and gesturing dramatically. Roy spoke some Spanish but when he got close enough to overhear their conversations they spoke so rapidly and without fully pronouncing most of their words that he could not understand anything they were saying.

Tina didn't like the Cuban girls. She was tall and blonde, as was her friend, LaDonna. When Roy asked Tina to dance she asked him what he thought of the Cuban girls. Before he could answer, Tina said, "They're cheap. They have big asses and dress like whores. LaDonna says her mother told her that their fathers have sex with them starting when they're five."

Roy found this hard to believe. He worked laying sewer pipe and shooting streets with Cuban men and liked them. They were good workers, glad to have a job, and they laughed a lot. Most of the time Roy didn't get their jokes—they spoke as rapidly as the girls at the dances—but they always offered to share their home-made lunches with Roy. He loved the Cuban food: lechon and pollo asado, platanos maduros, black beans and yellow rice.

Tina had blue eyes with yellow spots in them, an almost pretty face and a terrific figure. She and LaDonna wore as much or more make-up as the Cuban girls.

"Are you from around here?" Tina asked Roy. "You don't talk like you are."

"I'm from Chicago," he said. "I'm down here staying with my uncle for the summer."

"I'm almost seventeen," said Tina. "How old are you?"

"I'll be sixteen in October," Roy lied.

Tina was a little taller than Roy. She had slender, muscular arms and held him tightly, pulling him around during a slow dance. Her new breasts were as hard as her arms. She pushed herself against Roy and he got excited.

"I can tell you like me, Roy," Tina said, and smiled. Her teeth were crooked and up close Roy could see the pimples beneath cracks in her make-up.

Ralph was trying to get one of the Cuban girls to talk to him and LaDonna was dancing with a big, heavyset guy whose ears were perpendicular to his head. Tina told Roy that his name was Woody and that he was one of LaDonna's exes. "She's got a lot of 'em," Tina said.

After the slow dance Roy and Tina got cups of lemonade at the host table and stood off to the side.

"Do you want to walk me home?" Tina asked him. "I live four

blocks from here. I don't much like the music they're playing tonight and my parents make me come home early."

When they got to her house, a white, wooden bungalow set on concrete blocks with a wide front porch with a swing on it, Tina said, "Come in with me. My parents go to bed right after *Perry Mason* and then we can sneak out and go down to the river."

Tina introduced Roy to Ed and Irma, both of whom Tina addressed by their given names, not Mom and Dad, which Roy had never heard a kid do before. Ed and Irma sat in separate armchairs in the small livingroom watching Raymond Burr be a lawyer on their black and white Motorola. Roy and Tina sat slightly apart from each other on a lumpy couch. Ed and Irma did not say anything until the program was over. Ed stood up and turned off the television set after the theme music finished playing over the end credits.

"Man never loses a case," he said.

Ed had a huge belly and big arms. So did Irma. They both said goodnight and left the room. Tina put her right hand on Roy's left leg and squeezed his thigh. As soon as Tina heard the door to her parents' bedroom close and lock click, she turned to Roy and kissed him hard on the mouth.

Tina stood, took Roy's left hand and said, "Let's go down to the river and sit on the pier."

The river was at the end of Tina's street. She led him past a dwarf palm tree that was bent halfway over to a short pier and pulled him down onto the planks.

"Lie back," she said.

There were no boats moving on the water and except for insect noises it was quiet. Tina lay on top of Roy and rubbed her body against his. They kissed a few times with their mouths closed, then Tina rolled onto her side and with one hand unzipped his fly. Roy's cock popped up like a jack-in-the-box and Tina wrapped her right hand around it. He stared at the crescent moon as she stroked him slowly for a minute or so and then Roy tried to get up and lie on top of her. Tina pushed him back down, held him prostrate with her ropey arms, straddled his legs and put his cock into her mouth. Roy came immediately.

Tina rolled off of him and spat into the water, turned back to Roy and said, "You have a good dick, I think."

She stood up, so Roy did, too. He zipped up his pants. Tina had already begun walking back off the pier. They walked to her house without saying anything. Tina stopped in front of her porch steps. No lights were on. She stretched out her arms and rested them on Roy's shoulders.

"I won't be at the Cuban Club next Saturday," she said. "I'm going with Ed and Irma to Milwaukee on Monday. That's where Mamie, Irma's mother, lives. I have a cousin there, Ronnie. He's the only boy I let fuck me. He's twenty-one."

"How long have you been letting him do it?" Roy asked.

"Since a couple of months before my thirteenth birthday. This will be the fifth year. I only see Ronnie in the summer when we visit Mamie. Ronnie's getting married in September."

Tina kissed Roy on the mouth and this time she stuck her tongue in. Roy watched her go up the steps and into the house. He saw Irma sitting on the swing in the dark, smoking a cigarette.

"Go on now, boy," she said.

APPRECIATION

It was Roy's mother's third husband, Sid Wade, who told Roy that his father had died. Roy and Sid did not get along. Roy's mother had married Sid two years before, when Roy was ten, and it had since been obvious to Roy that if this husband had a choice, he would prefer Roy were not part of the deal.

Roy had gone home from school to have lunch and Sid took him into what had been Roy's grandfather's room before he moved to Florida to live with Roy's Uncle Buck. Ice coated the windows.

"Listen, Roy, your father died this morning," Sid said.

Roy knew his father was in the hospital being treated for colon cancer. He'd had an operation a few months before and needed to sit on a rubber pillow at the kitchen table. Also, since then Roy had seen his father's second wife, Evie, giving his dad shots with a large hypodermic needle. Despite the illness, Roy's father did not appear to have lost his strength or his sense of humor. The only difference Roy noticed was that his dad was at home more. Usually he was at his liquor store from early afternoon until three or four in the morning, and sometimes he didn't go home for twenty-four hours.

"In my business, there's always something going on," he told Roy. "If I don't pay attention, I'll end up paying in other ways, and if that happens too many times pretty soon I won't be in business."

There were always people coming in and going out of his dad's store, and men hanging around talking or whispering to each other or just standing and waiting. His dad seemed to know all of them and did not mind that none of them ever bought any liquor. The only times Roy saw a bottle of whiskey or gin change hands with one of them was when his dad gave it to him and did not ask for money. Sometimes a showgirl from the Club Alabam next door came in and without saying anything went down the rickety inside staircase into the basement with Roy's father. They would come back up a few minutes later and the girl would kiss his dad on his cheek and say, "Thanks a million, Rudy," or "You're a swell guy," before leaving. The showgirls came in on a break from rehearsals wearing only high heels and a skimpy costume under a coat. Roy thought they were all knockouts and he asked his father what they wanted to see him about.

"They need a little help from time to time, Roy," his dad said, "and I give them something to make 'em feel better."

"What do you give them?"

"It's not important, son. They're poor girls and I like to help people if I can."

"They always kiss you goodbye."

Roy's father smiled and said, "That's how they show their appreciation."

Roy wanted to go back to school in the afternoon after Sid Wade told him about his father, but Sid said he couldn't, that he would drive Roy to his father's house so he could be with Evie and his father's relatives. Roy asked his mother if he had to go to Evie's and she said yes, to show his respect. "She'll appreciate it," his mother said.

Years later, long after Sid Wade, his mother and Evie were dead, Roy, in recounting the events of that day for his own son, explained his asking to be allowed to go back to school as his desire to act normally, a way of denying to himself for the moment that his father was dead.

"I didn't really understand what it meant," Roy told his son, "that I'd never again see my father hanging out with his cronies or being kissed on the cheek by a showgirl from the Club Alabam. I wanted to help him and I couldn't."

"You help a lot of people now, though, Pop," Roy's son said. "Have you ever been kissed by a showgirl?"

THE AWFUL COUNTRY

When Roy's mother returned from her birthday trip with her companion Nicky Roznido, Roy asked her how it was and she said, "Everybody in Mexico carries a gun."

Roy was eight years old and his mother was twenty-nine for the second time. She didn't look thirty, she said to her friend Kay, and she saw no reason to admit to her real age until she absolutely had to.

"I was twenty-nine until two years ago," said Kay, "when I turned thirty-eight. I admitted it to Mario and he told me he didn't care so long as I looked good to him. I asked him what he would do when that day came and he said he'd have to buy a younger wife."

Kay and Roy's mother snickered and Roy, who was in the room with them, asked Kay, "Did Mario buy you?"

"He knew what he was getting when he married me," she said. "Be smart, Roy, don't ever get yourself into a situation where you're paying for more than you can afford."

"Cut it out, Kay," said Roy's mother. "He doesn't know what you're talking about."

Kay had flaming red hair and green eyes with black dust smudged around them. She was wearing a double strand of tiny pearls and diamond rings on the third fingers of both hands.

"Your mother's right, Roy," she said, and smiled, displaying more teeth than he could quickly count accurately. "Don't listen to me, it won't matter, anyway. Everyone makes their own mistakes."

Kay returned her attention to Roy's mother and said, "Come on, honey, I'm going to buy you a fancy lunch to celebrate your return from that awful country. Did Nicky have to shoot anybody this time?"

After Kay and his mother left the house, Roy went into his room and lay down on the bed. He could hear thunder but it was far away. He thought about what Kay had said about everyone making their own mistakes. He knew she meant something other than giving a wrong answer on a test. Roy remembered the morning his mother threw her second husband, Des Riley, out of the house. He was six then and his mother had said, "We won't have to listen to his bullcrap any more, Roy. That one was a mistake."

"Was my dad a mistake?" Roy asked her.

"No, Roy," she said, "I was just too young to know what I was doing."

His mother was really thirty now, not twenty-nine. How old did a person have to be to not be too young? If his father were still alive, Roy would ask him. It was not a question, he decided, that his mother could answer.

DEEP IN THE HEART

After she graduated from high school in Chicago, Roy's mother had gone to the University of Texas in Austin. When he was ten, Roy asked her why she had gone to college so far away.

"Your Uncle Buck was training to be a pilot at the Naval air station down there and he thought it would be a good idea for me to get away from the nuns and our mother. I was very shy. I'd spent ten years in boarding school being bossed around by the sisters and the priests, I'd never been on a date alone with a boy."

"Did you like Texas?"

"The girls were nice but sometimes they played tricks on me."

"What kinds of tricks?"

"Oh, one time at breakfast instead of two sunnyside up eggs they put two cow's eyes on my plate. But I liked how blue and enormous the sky was and singing 'Deep in the Heart of Texas' and 'The Eyes of Texas Are Upon You' at the football games."

"How long did you stay there?"

"Almost two years. My brother washed out of pilot school and got stationed in Philadelphia. He and Diana were married by then. My girlfriends talked me into entering a beauty contest at the university and I won. I was offered a modelling job in New York, so I went there and stayed with my Aunt Lorna and Uncle Dick."

"Aunt Lorna's the one I punched in the eye when I was two."

"That's right, when she came to Chicago to visit. She and Uncle

Dick had a beautiful house on 65th Street off Fifth Avenue. I was making my own money for the first time so I didn't see the point in going back to college."

"I got sick, though, so after a few months I came back to Chicago and spent a few weeks in the hospital being treated for a severe case of eczema. The doctors said I had a nervous condition and should avoid stress. Eventually I went back to work modelling furs for wholesale buyers in the showroom at the Merchandise Mart. I was only nineteen then. That's when I met your father. He was twenty years older and knew how to take care of me. Boys my own age didn't. So I married your dad and we honeymooned in Hollywood and Las Vegas. He arranged a screen test for me and his friends out there introduced me to some movie stars."

"Like who?"

"Oh, Errol Flynn and William Holden were the most famous ones. And that terrible Lawrence Tierney."

"What was terrible about him?"

"He was forward with me at the studio but then your dad's friends let him know the score and he apologized."

"I didn't know you could have been in the movies."

"I couldn't act, Roy, I didn't have any experience, so nothing came of it. Hollywood is full of pretty girls. I had fun, though. Your dad had business to do in Las Vegas so we spent quite a bit of time there. In those days everyone stayed at the El Rancho, it was the place to be before Ben opened his hotel."

"Who was Ben? Was he a friend of Dad's?"

"Yes. He was murdered in Los Angeles while we were with his girlfriend's brother in Vegas."

"Who killed him?"

"They never found out. When you're in business, it's easy to make enemies. People never know who their real friends are, anyway."

"I've got real friends."

Roy's mother smiled at him. She had beautiful teeth. They were sitting at the kitchen table and she patted him on his hand.

"Of course, Roy," she said. "I wasn't talking about you."

UNOPENED LETTERS

"Roy, would you please take out the placemats that are in the bottom drawer of the dining room dresser? The red ones underneath the candlesticks."

"Sure, Mom."

Roy's mother was preparing the house for a dinner party that evening in honor of her Aunt Lorna, who was visiting from New York. Roy was fifteen and had not encountered his great-aunt since he was about two years old, an occasion of which he had no recollection. Lorna had helped Roy's mother establish herself as a model in New York twenty-five years before and she had always been grateful to Lorna for her kindness and generosity; having a dinner party for Lorna during one of her rare visits to Chicago was the very least his mother could do.

"Ma, who's Frank Jameson?"

"What, Roy? Did you find the placemats?"

"Yes, but there was a marriage certificate and a bundle of unopened letters with a string tied around it underneath the placemats. The marriage certificate is between Nanny and a man named Frank Jameson. Who is he?"

Roy's mother came into the dining room and Roy handed her the certificate.

"And these letters all have a return address in Kansas City. They were sent to Nanny here in Chicago."

"The letters are from your grandfather to Nanny. She never opened them because she was married at the time to Frank Jameson."

"You mean that she and Pops got divorced? You never told me."

"No, Roy, I didn't think it was necessary for you to know. Maybe I was wrong not to tell you, but you and Pops were so close I didn't want anything to interfere with that."

"How long was Nanny married to Frank Jameson? You must have been a little girl then."

"Ten years, from when I was six to sixteen. He had a heart attack and died on Christmas day, just after my sixteenth birthday. Pops wanted to re-marry my mother but she didn't want to. He used to stand in a doorway across the street from our house and when she came out he'd try to talk to her. He'd gone to live in Kansas City after they divorced, then he moved back to Chicago after Frank died. Pops still loved Nanny and wrote her letters but she wouldn't open them. Half of those letters he sent while Frank was still alive."

"But she lived for twelve years after Frank Jameson died, until you were twenty-eight. Why didn't she open them for all those years?"

"I don't know. I only discovered them after Nanny died. I didn't want to just throw them away."

"Did you tell Pops you had them?"

"No. I meant to but I never did. I don't know why exactly except that because of things my mother said I blamed Pops for breaking up their marriage. And after he died, I hid them away."

"Along with Nanny's marriage certificate to Frank Jameson. You grew up with him, Ma. Did you like him? What was his profession? And why did Pops and Nanny get divorced?"

"Frank was all right to me but not to my brother. I was sent away to boarding school, so I didn't spend much time with him. He didn't want anything to do with your Uncle Buck, and since Buck was fourteen years older than me he was already pretty much on his own. The Jameson family were fairly well-to-do. They were Irish, the father and mother were born in County Kerry, and there were four brothers, including Frank. They owned warehouses in and around Chicago. Frank was a devout Catholic, so Nanny began going to church regularly. She became close friends with the Mother Superior at St. Theresa's, near where we lived."

"She was in our house a lot when Nanny was dying. I remember her. I'd never seen a woman with a mustache before. What about Pops and Nanny? Why did they split up?"

"Pops had a girlfriend, Sally Carmel, who lived in Kansas City. I guess he met her on one of his business trips. He still loved Nanny, though, and wanted her to go back with him. I think that's what's in those letters."

"Love letters."

"I suppose."

"Are you ever going to open them?"

"I don't know. Perhaps it's better to leave them unopened. They're addressed to my mother, not to me. I've often wondered why she kept them. I should probably burn them."

Roy's mother replaced the letters and the marriage certificate in the bottom drawer of the dresser and closed it.

"Let's not talk about this any more now, Roy. I've got to have everything ready for the dinner. Aunt Lorna will be here at five."

She went into the kitchen. Roy sat down on a chair in the dining room and looked out the window. The sky was gray with black specks in it, a snow sky. He wondered what else his mother thought was unnecessary for him to know.

Walking to St. Tim's the next morning, Roy asked his friend

Johnny McLaughlin if he thought either or both of his parents kept secrets about their family from him and his brothers.

"The Catholic church is all about secrets," said Johnny. "It's the mysteries keep people comin' back for more, hopin' they'll some day get filled in on the real goods. My Uncle Sean is always goin' on about the Rosetta stone, you know, that hunk of rock found in Egypt over a hundred years ago has pictures of birds and half-moons on it symbolize something important. My parents ain't no different. They just tell me and Billy and Jimmy what's necessary to keep us in line. Only the dead know the meaning of existence, and they don't answer letters."

"They don't even open them," said Roy.

CHICAGO, ILLINOIS, 1953

Roy and his mother had come back to Chicago from Cuba by way of Key West and Miami so that she could attend the funeral of her Uncle Ike, her father's brother. Roy was six years old and though he would not be going to the funeral—he'd stay at home with his grandmother, who was too ill to attend—he looked forward to seeing Pops, his grandfather, during his and his mother's time in the city.

It was mid-February and the weather was at its most miserable. The temperature was close to zero, ice and day-old snow covered the streets and sidewalks, and sharp winds cut into pedestrians from several directions at once. Had it not been out of fondness and respect for her father's brother, Roy's mother would never have ventured north from the tropics at this time of year. Uncle Ike had always been especially kind and attentive to his niece and Roy's mother was sincerely saddened by his passing.

She and Roy had first stopped on the way in from the airport to see Roy's father, from whom his mother had recently been divorced, at his liquor store, and were now in a taxi on their way to Roy's grandmother's house when she told the driver to stop so that she could buy something at a pharmacy.

"Wait here in the cab, Roy," she said, "it's warmer. I'll only be a couple of minutes."

Roy watched his mother tiptoe gingerly across the frozen sidewalk and enter the drugstore. The taxi was parked on Ojibway Avenue, which Roy recognized was not very far from his grandmother's neighborhood.

"That your mother?" the driver asked.

"Yes."

"She's a real attractive lady. You live in Chicago?"

"Sometimes," said Roy. "My grandmother lives here. Right now we live in Havana, Cuba, and Key West, Florida."

"You live in both places?"

"We go back and forth on the ferry. They're pretty close."

"Your parents got two houses, huh?"

"They're divorced. My mom and I live in hotels."

"You like that, livin' in hotels?"

"We've always lived in hotels, even when my mom and dad were married. I was born in one in Chicago."

"Where's your dad live?"

"Here, mostly. Sometimes he's in Havana or Las Vegas."

"What business is he in?"

Roy was getting anxious about his mother. The rear window on his side of the cab kept steaming up and Roy kept wiping it off.

"My mother's been in there a long time," he said. "I'm going in to find her."

"Hold on, kid, she'll be right back. The drugstore's probably crowded."

Roy opened the curbside door and said, "Don't drive away. My mom'll pay you."

He got out and went into the drugstore. His mother standing in front of the cash counter. Three or four customers in line were behind her.

"You dumb son of a bitch!" his mother shouted at the man standing behind the counter. "How dare you talk to me like that!"

52

The clerk was tall and slim and he was wearing wire-rim glasses and a brown sweater.

"I told you," he said, "we don't serve Negroes. Please leave the store or I'll call the police."

"Go on, lady," said a man standing in line. "Go someplace else."

"Mom, what's wrong?" Roy said.

The customers and the clerk looked at him.

"This horrible man refuses to wait on me because he thinks I'm a Negro."

"But you're not a Negro," Roy said.

"It doesn't matter if I am or not. He's stupid and rude."

"Is that your son?" the clerk asked.

"He's white," said a woman in the line. "He's got a suntan but he's a white boy."

"I'm sorry, lady," said the clerk, "it's just that your skin is so dark."

"Her hair's red," said the woman. "She and the boy have been in the sun too much down south somewhere."

Roy's mother threw the two bottles of lotion she'd been holding at the clerk. He caught one and the other bounced off his chest and fell on the floor behind the counter.

"Come on, Roy, let's get out of here," said his mother.

The taxi was still waiting with the motor running and they got in. The driver put it into gear and pulled away from the curb.

"You get what you needed, lady?" he asked.

"Mom, why didn't you tell the man that you aren't a Negro?"

Roy's mother's shoulders were shaking and tears were running down her cheeks. He could see her hands trembling as she wiped her face.

"Because it shouldn't matter, Roy. This is Chicago, Illinois, not Birmingham, Alabama. It's against the law not to serve Negroes."

"No it ain't, lady," said the driver.

"It should be," said Roy's mother.

"How could they think you're black?" the driver said. "If I'd thought you were a Negro, I wouldn't have picked you up."

THE COLONY OF THE SUN

Gina Crow played Hoagy Carmichael records every Saturday morning. Certain records she played more than once. One day Roy heard "Hong Kong Blues" and "Old Man Harlem" twice, and "Memphis in June" three times. Usually, the last song Mrs. Crow played was "Stardust". All of these versions featured Hoagy Carmichael with solo piano, except for "New Orleans", on which he sang a duet with a woman. Roy liked to sit on his back porch from about eight to nine o'clock listening to the records during the year Gina Crow and her daughter, Polly, lived next door. Polly was twelve, a year older than Roy. She had cat's eyes, billiard ball black with yellow flames in the center. Polly looked and acted older than she was, and she had a sharp-edged manner of speaking that made her sound mean or angry. She made Roy feel uncomfortable but excited at the same time.

"Martha Poole told me that Gina Crow's husband is getting out of prison."

"I didn't know she had a husband."

"Martha said he was busted in Toledo, where they used to live."

"What for?"

"Embezzlement. She thinks he worked in a bank."

Roy's mother and her husband were washing and drying dishes while Roy was sitting at the kitchen table eating a bowl of cereal.

"What's embezzlement?" he asked.

55

"It means he stole money," said his mother.

"Is he coming to live with them?" her husband asked.

"Martha doesn't know."

"If he's on probation, he'll have to stay in Ohio. For a while, anyway."

"I'm just glad he didn't rape or murder anyone. I wouldn't feel comfortable having a murderer living next door to us."

Walking home from school the next day, Roy was following behind Polly Crow and her friend Vida when he heard Polly say that her father was coming home soon, and that she had not seen him for a long time.

"Where's he been?" asked Vida.

"Far away, in the Colony of the Sun."

"I've never heard of that place. Is it in the United States?"

"I think it might be in Canada, or Antarctica."

"What was he doing there?"

"Working on a big project. My mother told me he was exploring for something that could save the planet."

"You mean Earth?"

"Yeah. My mother says pretty soon there won't be enough coal to heat all of our houses."

"Maybe he was digging oil wells. They use oil to heat houses, too."

"Could be. She says the men there have to shoot polar bears and seals to have meat."

After Vida turned off at her street and Polly was by herself, Roy caught up to her and said hello.

"Oh, hi, Roy. Were you walking behind me and Vida?"

"Yes. I heard what you said about your father being in Antarctica."

"It gets even colder there than here in Chicago. We might move to New Orleans, where it's a lot warmer. My mother lived there when she was a little girl."

Polly was taller than Roy. She had long brown hair and very white skin. The wind blew her hair across her face and she kept pushing it back into place.

"How long has it been since you've seen him?"

"I was eight. We were in Toledo then."

"I like the records your mother plays. Sometimes I sit on our porch and listen to them."

Polly stopped walking and turned and faced Roy. Her lips were purple and she brushed her hair out of her eyes.

"Two nights ago my mother got drunk on vodka and told me my father isn't my real father, and that my real father was a boy named Bobby Boles and that he was killed in a bar fight in Houston, Texas. At least that's what she heard because he abandoned her when she told him she was pregnant. She married my father when I was a year old. She told me she still loved Bobby Boles, even though he was dead, and that every time she looks at me she sees him in my face and it makes her want to cry."

Roy stared at the jumpy yellow flames in Polly Crow's eyes. They got bigger, then smaller, then big again.

"She never told you this before?"

Polly shook her head. The wind whipped her hair around.

"Why do you think she wanted you to know now?"

"She made me promise not to tell my father that she told me. She said Bobby Boles had been her sister's boyfriend, my Aunt Earlene, who's older and lives in Little Rock, Arkansas. I've never met her. My mother says when Earlene found out Bobby Boles fucked my mother she called her a whore and swore she'd never speak to her again, and she hasn't."

Roy had never heard a girl say fuck before. Polly started to walk, so he did, too. She didn't say anything else and when they got to her house Polly went in without saying goodbye.

As far as Roy knew, Gina Crow's husband never showed up, and a few months after Polly had told Roy about her real father she and her mother moved away without telling Roy or his mother and her husband or Martha Poole to where.

"Gina's an odd woman," Roy's mother said one night at the dinner table. "Her daughter, too. She'll be trouble when she grows up, if she's not already. Where do you suppose they went?"

"The Colony of the Sun," said Roy.

"There's no such place," said his mother's husband.

CREEPS

Roy noticed the creepy little guy following him right after he got off the bus. Roy was on his way to the Riviera theater to see a double feature of *The Alligator People* and *First Man Into Space*. His friends Buzzy Riordan and Jimmy Boyle were meeting him there. Buzzy had once been thrown out of the Riviera for shouting "Fire!" and ordered never to return, but that had been more than a year before so he figured the manager and the ushers wouldn't recognize him, especially since he now had a crewcut and was taller. Buzzy told Roy he'd done it so that he could get a better seat; he'd gotten to the theater late and all the seats except for ones in the first row were taken and he hated sitting so close to the screen because he had to look up all the time and the actors' heads were too small. Lots of kids ran out into the lobby and Buzzy moved back and sat down in the center seat of a middle row. When the kid who had been sitting there came back after learning it was a false alarm told Buzzy to move Buzzy told him to get lost. The kid called an usher and a girl who'd been sitting in the front row near Buzzy and was now walking back to her seat pointed at him and said, "That's the creep who yelled fire!"

Buzzy and Jimmy Boyle were in the same fifth grade class at Delvis Erland grammar school, which most of the kids called Devil's Island. The grades went from kindergarten through eighth so if a student spent the entire time there he or she could say that they'd done nine years of hard labor at Devil's Island. The school had been built in 1902 and resembled an asylum or prison out of Victorian England. When Roy saw the movie of *Jane Eyre* on TV he thought the similarity between Lowood Institute and Devil's Island was unmistakable.

The creep who was following Roy was very short, no more than five feet tall, with splotchy bleached blonde hair, a frog-faced kisser and a pudgy build. Roy guessed his age at about forty. The man trailed Roy from the bus stop toward the theater, keeping a few feet behind him. Roy hurried but did not run, hoping that Buzzy and Jimmy would be in front of the Riv waiting for him.

Roy had to wait across the street from the theater for the light to change. He saw his friends standing under the marquee sharing a smoke. Before Roy stepped off the curb the creep was standing next to him.

"Hello, sonny," he said, "are you hungry? I'd like to buy you a hamburger."

Just then the light changed to green and Roy ran over to Buzzy and Jimmy.

"Hey Roy," said Buzzy, "we thought maybe you weren't comin'. *The Alligator People*'s gonna start."

"Yeah," Jimmy said, "Buzzy was just sayin' how if we couldn't get good seats right away he'd have to yell 'Fire!' again."

"Uh uh, I was gonna shout 'Rat!'"

When the blonde babe in *The Alligator People* who's wandering lost in a spooky southern swamp sees that her husband has turned partly into a gator, she screams, reminding Roy of the creep with bleached hair who had followed him on the street. The skin on the creep's face was scaly looking, like an alligator's, and his hair was almost as long as the actress's. Roy hoped the guy wouldn't be waiting for him outside the theater when he got out. Buzzy and Jimmy would be with him, though, so he figured the creep wouldn't try anything. The boys would stay for both movies unless Buzzy pulled some stunt that would get the three of them tossed before *First Man Into Space* was over. The show wouldn't let out until dark. Roy was sure the creep would have found another boy to follow around by then.

ACHILLES AND THE BEAUTIFUL LAND

Roy enjoyed listening to the old guy who fixed zippers tell stories. The man would come through the back door into the kitchen of Roy's house and sit down on the rickety little wooden chair with the left rear leg that was a quarter of an inch shorter than its other three. Roy's mother kept the crooked chair because it had belonged to her grandmother and when his mother was a little girl she would sit on it. A daffodil had been painted in yellow on the inside back of the chair but it had faded badly over the years and Roy knew the vague shape was once a daffodil only because his mother told him so. Roy asked her why one leg was shorter than the others and she said she didn't really know but that her grandmother had owned a brown and white mutt named Blackie who liked to chew on the chair's legs; teeth marks, presumably Blackie's, decorated all four of them.

The man who fixed zippers called himself Achilles. He was eighty-eight years old, he said, when he first appeared at the back door and asked Roy's mother if she had any zippers that needed repairing. He spoke English but with a strange accent punctuated by a cloudy cough that sometimes made it difficult for Roy to understand him. Roy was five when he met Achilles, who remained a regular visitor for more than a year. Even when there were no zippers on Roy's mother's dresses or jackets to fix Achilles would come in and sit on the crooked chair by the door and talk to her and Roy, often telling stories about his childhood in a place he called the beautiful land. The beautiful land, said Achilles, was in another country, much smaller than America, a half-step from the Orient, where he had been born. Roy asked him what the name of the country was but Achilles said he didn't know any more; the country had been invaded by soldiers from many other countries over the years and each time the name had been changed. The old man preferred to recall it only as the beautiful land, describing the forests and rivers and hills and villages where a boy such as he had been was welcomed into any hut or house to eat or sleep.

"Why did you leave there?" Roy asked him.

"When an army wearing helmets sporting blue feathers arrived from the East everyone in every village was forced to abandon their homes and belongings and march together for many days and nights to a train station. I was thirteen years old then and I had never seen a train, so I was curious, and even though I did not want to leave the beautiful land, I did not really mind going. I had heard people describe trains and when I finally saw one I was thrilled that I was going to ride on it. The train was puffing white smoke and hissing like a big long dragon."

"Where did it take you?"

"Far away from the beautiful land to a place I have forgotten."

"Did your parents bring you to Chicago?"

"My parents were made to travel on a different train. One day I did not see them and ever since there has been another day."

"What kinds of animals were there in the beautiful land?"

"Deer, tigers and birds, and fish, of course, in the rivers and lakes."

"Didn't the tigers eat the deer?"

"Yes, Roy, and hunters killed and ate both of them, as well as the fish."

"Did the tigers ever eat the people who lived in the villages?"

"A tiger once spoke to me. I was walking in the woods, looking for mushrooms, when a magnificent orange and black and white beast appeared in my path."

"How old were you?"

"No more than ten. I was a small boy, only a bit bigger than you are now."

"You're still small, Achilles. For a grown man, I mean."

"Being small has its advantages. I assumed the tiger was going to eat me but he just stared with his yellow eyes and said, 'Come back when you are larger and will make a better meal.' Then he disappeared into the trees."

Roy told his mother that a tiger had spoken to Achilles and she said, "That was in a time when people and animals were still polite to one another."

"Achilles said the tiger wouldn't eat him because he was too small."

"That's what I mean," she said.

Roy did not see Achilles for a while so he asked his mother if she had.

"No, Achilles has gone back to the beautiful land. He told me to tell you that he looks forward to seeing you there in about a hundred years."

"Can you show me on a map where the beautiful land is?"

"Achilles said, 'Tell Roy that when the time comes he'll know how to get there. I'll be waiting for him.'"

"A hundred years is a long time to wait," said Roy.

"Maybe not," said his mother, "not if you're in the beautiful land. Achilles won't ever leave there again."

MEN IN THE KITCHEN

"So you were already in the basement when this man attacked you."

"Yes, I was doing the laundry."

"You didn't hear him approaching?"

"No, the washing machine was filling with water. I'd just put in a second load, and I was putting the wet things from the first load into the dryer, so I couldn't hear over the noise."

"Do you always leave the basement door open when you're doing laundry?"

"Yes, to have some fresh air, unless it's cold and raining or snowing. The ventilation down there isn't very good, and it was a warm, sunny day."

"You were loading up the dryer. Then what happened?"

"A hand came over my mouth and he wrapped his other arm around my chest. The knife was in his left hand."

"Left-handed. Go on."

"The man said, 'Don't try to scream or I'll cut your throat.' Then he dragged me away from the washing machine and dryer into the passageway by the storage area. He forced me to the ground and took his hands away. That's when he saw that I'm pregnant and cursed."

"What did he say exactly?"

"God damn it. He said it three or four times. I kept saying, 'Don't hurt my baby, don't hurt my baby.' He took out a piece of rope and cut it with his knife, then turned me onto my left side, facing away from him, and tied my hands behind my back. He told me to shut up and I heard him making sounds."

"What kinds of sounds?"

"I think he was masturbating."

"How long did this go on?"

"You mean his masturbating?"

"Yes."

"It couldn't have been for very long, maybe a minute or two."

"You didn't scream or call for help?"

"He would have stabbed me or cut my throat if I had, I'm sure of it. When he was finished he walked out of the basement, out the back door. He didn't run. I didn't try to look at him, I didn't want to see his face. I stayed on the ground for several minutes before I got to my feet. It was difficult because my balance isn't good. I'm in my eighth month."

"It sounds like the same guy who attacked the other women. None of them were pregnant."

"Did he rape them?"

"Yes, ma'am. He cut one."

"Did she die?"

"No, she's recovering."

"Nobody could recover from that."

Roy's mother and two men were seated at the kitchen table when he came home from school. Roy stood and looked at the men, both of whom were wearing coats and ties and hats and were clean shaven. One of them wore glasses and the other had a bluish scar on the right side of his chin.

"Hi, Mom," he said, "are these guys friends of Dad's?"

She hugged him and said to the men, "This is my son, Roy. He's seven."

"Hello, son," said the man wearing glasses.

"No, Roy," said his mother, "they're detectives. They're investigating a case, something that happened nearby. They're asking me if I know anything about it."

"Do you?" Roy asked.

"The boy wasn't home when it happened?" said the man with the scar.

"No, he was at school."

The detectives stood up.

"We'll get back to you about this. Are you sure you don't want to go to the hospital?"

"No, I'm all right. I'll call my doctor myself."

"Thank you for your cooperation, ma'am," said the man wearing glasses.

"We'll find our way out," said the other detective.

The men left and Roy sat down in the chair in which the man with the blue scar had been sitting.

"Mom, are you okay? Why did they ask if you wanted to go to the hospital?"

"They were being kind because I'm pregnant."

"Can I help you with anything?"

"Not now, sweetheart. I'm going to take a sponge bath and then I've got to finish the laundry. You can help me carry the baskets upstairs when it's dry."

"What kind of case are they investigating?"

Roy's mother placed her hands flat on the table and pushed herself up.

"I'll tell you later," she said, "How was school today?"

ANNA LOUISE

Roy's cousin Skip's mother, Anna Louise, was an alcoholic. The first thing she did every morning after she got out of bed was go into the kitchen and put a teaspoon of sugar into a chimney size glass, fill it with gin, stir it up and drink half of it. Then she lit a gold-papered, unfiltered cigarette and took a long drag before finishing off her glass of gin. She was a natural platinum blonde with unblemished ghost-white skin. Anna Louise was Roy's Uncle Buck's first wife; after him, she married Karl von Sydow, a Swedish construction magnate. Von Sydow died of a heart attack six years after marrying Anna Louise and left his fortune to her. She and Skip, who was fifteen when von Sydow died, lived north of Chicago on an estate fronted by a high brick wall. A stream ran through thick woods that bordered the other three sides of the property. Anna Louise owned the land the woods and stream were on. She was forty-two and still beautiful when her second husband died. After she'd drunk the glassful of gin, she puffed on her cigarette for a minute or two before returning to the bathroom that adjoined the master bedroom and began running water into the sunken tub. She remained entirely nude during this routine no matter who else was in the house. Roy was thirteen when he first witnessed his aunt's diurnal performance. Anna Louise had perfect posture, having as a girl and young woman been a dancer and an actress before working briefly as a teacher of calculus and poetry at a private girls' school. She was twenty-two when she married Roy's uncle, who, Anna Louise unembarrassedly informed Roy, had not been her first lover, though she had let him believe so.

"Your uncle was good to me and an ardent paramour," she said, "until he impregnated me. After that, I seldom saw him. It wasn't much of a marriage. Von Sydow was consistently hands on, shall I say. I don't know which was worse. I should have married a Jew."

Roy's aunt delivered this information to him while he and his cousin Skip were seated at the breakfast table eating cereal, the only food Anna Louise kept in the house. She had yet to run her bath.

Roy saw her infrequently during his teenage years, the last time being when he was seventeen and she was living in a motel in an unfashionable suburb of the city. This was after she had unintentionally set fire to her house, which burned to the ground. Anna Louise had passed out drunk in her bedroom, where firemen found her collapsed on the floor and carried her out just before the roof caved in.

According to Skip, most of his mother's money was gone, swindled by von Sydow's attorney whom she had trusted to manage her financial affairs, and she spent the majority of her waking hours drinking gin out of the bottle from a case on the floor next to her bed positioned so that to extract a new bottle all she had to do was reach down and lift it up to her lips.

The last Roy heard of Anna Louise was that she had been admitted to an assisted living facility in Indiana, where she had relatives. By that time, however, her mind was gone, as well as what little money she had left, and she died sober and fully dressed sitting in a wheelchair. Skip was overseas in the army at the time and did not come back for the funeral, which was paid for by his father.

MULES IN THE WILDERNESS

Bruno and Lily had moved to a new house since Roy had last seen them, which had been at the funeral of Grandpa Joseph, his dad and Bruno's father, five years before, when Roy was fourteen. Roy's uncle and aunt had not made an effort to keep in touch with him since his dad died, two years before the death of Grandpa Joseph. Roy had been living in Europe for the last two years and was visiting his mother in Chicago before continuing on to the West Coast. He decided to stop by Bruno and Lily's just to say hello and see their house. He had always liked his aunt Lily, a lively, attractive woman who at one time had been quite friendly with his mother, even after his parents divorced. "Give my best to Lily," Roy's mother said to him.

Bruno was another story, as were Roy's cousins Daria and Delilah. Daria was a year younger than Roy and Delilah five years younger. Ever since Roy could remember both Daria and her father seemed always to be in a bad mood, and Delilah uncommunicative, keeping very much to herself. Roy's mother told him that his Uncle Bruno had wanted sons, not daughters, and made his feelings obvious in his behavior toward Daria and Delilah; he remained cold and distant, leaving Lily with the responsibility of raising them. Besides this and catering to her husband, Lily devoted much of her time to work on behalf of Mother Wolfram's Mission for the Misshapen and other charitable organizations.

When his uncle answered the front door, he did so by peering through a narrow slit. Not recognizing Roy, he asked who he was. Roy identified himself, which caused Bruno to pause for several seconds before informing him that there were too many locks to undo on the door and instructing him to come around the side of the house where he would be admitted through the servants' entrance.

It was Lily who admitted him. She smiled and seemed pleased to see Roy. His aunt had worn heavy pancake makeup ever since he'd known her and dark red, precisely applied lipstick so Roy was not surprised when she air-kissed him on both sides of his face. Lily guided Roy up a winding staircase and through an enormous kitchen into a den that he could see connected to a livingroom. Daria and Delilah, she informed him, were away at boarding school in the East. Bruno was sitting in a high-backed chair and motioned with his right index finger for Roy to sit in an armchair across from him.

"Is your mother still alive?" Lily asked.

"She is," said Roy.

"Say hello to her for me," his aunt said, then left the room.

Roy looked around. There were paintings on the walls of older men in suits, none of whom Roy recognized.

"What do you want?" asked Bruno.

Roy's father's only brother was a large man, a couple of inches over six feet tall and he weighed in excess of 220 pounds. Bruno wore his pants fastened just below his chest, a blue dress shirt and dark brown tie; he had a bushy mustache and a full head of gray-brown hair that stood up like a stiff brush.

"I came to say hello to you and Aunt Lily," said Roy. "I've been living abroad for two years."

"Do you plan to stay in Chicago now?"

"No, I'm on my way to California."

Bruno was an auctioneer; he handled sales of restaurants, automobile dealerships, private estates and business properties. Roy recalled his mother once commenting that Bruno could for the right price acquire anything anyone wanted. He was Roy's father's older brother by four years but he seemed to Roy to belong to an earlier time, a Biblical epoch when kings ruled unchallenged. Bruno scrutinized his nephew as if Roy were a freak in a carnival.

"I can have the maid make you a sandwich if you're hungry," he said.

Roy shook his head. "Who are the men in these paintings?"

"Mules in the wilderness, ones who survived."

Roy and his uncle sat in silence until Roy stood up.

"Use the servants' door," said Bruno.

When Roy returned to his mother's house she asked him if he'd seen Bruno and Lily.

"Lily says hello. She wasn't sure you were still alive."

"Does she still look the same?"

"Like a Kabuki actress," said Roy. "She still wears more makeup than Lon Chaney."

"What did Bruno have to say?"

"He asked me what I wanted."

"And what did you tell him?"

"Nothing. We didn't talk much. He asked me if I was hungry. He said the maid could make me a sandwich."

Roy's mother was sitting on a couch in the livingroom. Roy sat down in a chair on the opposite side of the coffee table.

"You know that was my father's favorite chair," she said.

"I remember Pops sitting in it in the afternoons reading the *Daily News* when I came home from school. I sat on the floor next to him and he read to me from the sports section."

Rain streaked the windows behind Roy's mother.

"Looks like I got home just in time," he said.

"When your father died he didn't leave a will. Intestate, it's called. He left Bruno in charge of all of his affairs, but he told me you would be taken care of. Bruno said your dad didn't have anything to leave, that he had to pay off his brother's debts and there was nothing left for you. My brother knew Bruno was lying and so did I. Your dad kept money in safe deposit boxes in hotels and God knows where else. He didn't want the government to know what he had and he never trusted the banks. Your Uncle Buck talked to Bruno about it but there was nothing he could do. If your dad left a will my guess is that Bruno burned it."

"Why didn't you tell me this before?"

"You were twelve years old, there wasn't any point. What was done was done."

"He acted like I'd come there to kill him."

Roy's mother gave a little laugh. "Bruno was afraid of you, that you knew he'd stolen whatever your father had."

"Did Aunt Lily know?"

"Bruno never told her anything about his business."

A year after Roy saw his uncle, Bruno died. In a letter Roy's mother told him an article in the *Chicago Tribune* said the police suspected foul play, that Bruno had been poisoned and that Daria and Delilah were being held in protective custody on suspicion of murdering their father. In her next letter Roy's mother enclosed a newspaper clipping featuring a photograph of Lily that said she had committed suicide by ingesting an overdose of sleeping pills and that she had left a note confessing that she, not her daughters, had poisoned her husband. Her estate, she instructed, should be divided equally between her children and Mother Wolfram's Mission for the Misshapen.

In her second letter Roy's mother wrote, "Your dad told me that when he was four years old and Bruno was eight, Bruno hammered a nail through one of his fingers into a piece of wood on purpose to test himself to see if he could do it and not cry. I asked your dad if Bruno cried and he said yes but that his brother promised him if he told anyone he would nail your father's fingers to a tree."

THE BOY WHOSE MOTHER MAY HAVE MARRIED A LEOPARD ·

When he was eight years old Roy had a dream in which his mother, who in real life had already been married three times, came home one day with a leopard and told Roy that the leopard was her new husband. The leopard was very big and he was not tawny but black with even darker spots that could be seen only if a person looked closely at his skin.

"How could you marry a leopard, Mom?" Roy asked. "I didn't know that human beings and animals could marry each other."

In the dream Roy's mother did not answer his question. The following morning when he told her his dream she laughed and said, "I may have married a leopard when I was younger, before you were born. I can't remember, my memory's not so good about those things."

"You'd remember if you married a leopard."

"Did I have him on a leash?"

"I don't think so."

"Figures." she said.

Walking to school Roy told his friend Jimmy Boyle about his dream and Jimmy said, "Nobody would ever pick on a kid if they knew his old man was a leopard."

Roy did not like the men his mother married. His real father had died when Roy was three years old, so he had not really known him, but Roy convinced himself that these other husbands were different. Maybe, he thought, the leopard in the dream was how he wanted his real father to have been, powerful and beautiful, someone who would always be there to protect him.

A few days later Roy's mother's friend Kay, who wore a lot of make-up and whose bright red lipstick was always slightly smeared, said to him, "Kitty told me you had a dream that she'd married a wild beast."

"A leopard," said Roy.

"It was a symbol," Kay said.

"What's that?"

"Something that represents something else, like a desire or a feeling you didn't know you had. I've got lots of repressed desires. My doctor says it's why my skin breaks out."

"Don't confuse him, Kay," said Roy's mother.

Kay was holding a lit cigarette in her right hand; she ran the fingers of her left hand through Roy's hair.

"Your father had thick dark hair like yours," she said.

Roy saw an old black and white movie on TV in which a black leopard escapes from a zoo and turns into a woman who gets hit by a car and dies but before she does she turns back into a leopard. He told Jimmy Boyle about it and Jimmy asked him if he ever had the dream again about his mother marrying a leopard.

Roy shook his head. "No, it probably got run over, too."

A few months later Roy overheard his mother telling someone on the telephone that Kay had divorced her husband and married one of his mother's ex-husbands, but that had not worked out so Kay was going to divorce him, too. Not long after this Roy came home and found Kay and his mother sitting in the livingroom drinking highballs, smoking cigarettes and talking.

"Hello, Roy," said Kay, "how nice to see you. What are you doing with yourself these days? "

"Playing baseball and going to school. What are you doing?"

Kay puffed on her cigarette. Her lipstick was smeared more than usual.

"Waiting for you to grow up," she said.

STUNG

When Roy's mother swam into a bevy of jellyfish and got stung by them he was walking along the beach smashing men-of-war with a board. He liked hearing them pop and seeing their blue ink spurt onto the white sand. Roy took care to stand a couple of feet away from the cephalopods, not wanting to step on their invisible poisonous tentacles. He heard his mother's screams and saw her walking unsteadily out of the ocean. She was crying and two teen-age girls who were sunbathing on the beach got up and ran over to her. Roy dropped the board and ran over, too.

"It was terrible," his mother said, sobbing between words. "I was swimming close to shore and all of a sudden I was surrounded by jellyfish. They stuck to my back and I couldn't get away from them. They kept stinging me."

"Jesus, lady, your back is full of wounds, your shoulders, too," said one of the girls. "You should see a doctor right away."

"They're hairs," said the other girl. "The stingers are actually hairs that grow out of their tentacles. I learned it in biology."

Roy and his mother were in Miami Beach, staying at the Delmonico Hotel, waiting for his father to come over on the ferry from Havana. Roy knew that his parents were getting a divorce but he didn't know exactly what it meant. He understood that his father would not be living with him and his mother any more, but his dad had seldom been with them in the past few months anyway, so Roy didn't think that would make much of a difference.

At the doctor's office, Roy was made to sit in the waiting room while his mother was being attended to. A receptionist asked him how old he was and when he told her five but almost six she gave him six Tootsie Rolls. Roy didn't like Tootsie Rolls but he took them from her anyway, said thank you, and stuffed them in the right hand pocket of his silver-blue Havana Kings jacket.

Later, Roy decided, he would distribute them to the bus boys at the Delmonico. Roy had gotten to know them well during the five weeks he and his mother had been there. They had all been nice to him—especially Leo, Chi Chi, Chico and Alberto—giving him dishes of ice cream and Coca-Colas while he hung out in the hotel kitchen and talked to them about baseball. They were all Cubans and Roy often went to the Sugar Kings games with his father when he was in Havana. In December, Roy's father had introduced him to El Vaquero, "The Cowboy," the Cuban League home run champion who had for many years played third base for the Cienfuegos team. El Vaquero, whose real name was Raimundo Pardo, had recently had "una taza de café" with the Washington Senators, but he'd struck out much more often than he'd hit home runs for them so the Senators had cut him loose. El Vaquero was going to play now for the Sugar Kings. Roy was looking forward to seeing him hit home runs out of Gran Stadium, but when he told this to Chico and Leo they laughed and said El Vaquero was too old, that his nickname should be changed to El Viejo, "The Old Guy."

"What did the doctor do, Mom?" Roy asked when they were in a taxi going back to the hotel.

"He washed and disinfected the places where I was stung and then applied ointment to them. He said they'll take a few days to heal. You'll rub the ointment on my back for me at night, won't you, Roy?"

"Sure, if you want me to. But I go to sleep before you do. When Dad gets here, he can do it if I'm already in bed."

Roy's mother looked out the cab's window on her side. The sidewalks were very crowded and the taxi couldn't go fast because a wagon filled with plantains being pulled by a horse was in front of it.

"Don't talk about your dad," she said. "Not right now."

"Why, Mom? He's coming to Miami, isn't he?"

"It hurts, Roy. I didn't think it would, but it does."

"Don't worry, Mom, they're just jellyfish stings. You'll be okay in a few days."

EL ALMUERZO POR POCO

The girl was sitting at a corner table next to a window, gently knocking ash from her cigarette into an empty cup. The café was crowded due to the rain; nobody wanted to leave until it stopped or at least let up a bit. Customers were standing, holding cups and saucers and plates in their hands, ready to pounce if a table became free. She didn't want to give up hers, even though she had finished her coffee.

Roy was with his mother having a quick lunch before her appointment at the dermatologist's. After both of them had ordered grilled cheese sandwiches and coconut milkshakes, Roy's mother told him that she had to make a phone call. He had noticed the girl in the corner as soon as they'd sat down and now could hardly take his eyes off of her. She was about seventeen or eighteen, Roy guessed. Her thick black hair fell over one eye but he thought she looked a lot like Elizabeth Taylor in the movie *Suddenly, Last Summer,* which he'd seen the day before with his mother. Roy was twelve years old and a sign at the theater had said No Minors Allowed but his mother had bought two tickets anyway and nobody tried to stop him from going in with her. After they'd taken their seats, Roy whispered to his mother that children weren't supposed to see the movie.

"It's a matinee, Roy," she whispered back to him. The theater's not even half full. They're just glad to sell tickets."

When the girl at the corner table leaned back in her chair and brushed the hair off of her face, Roy felt a little flutter in his stomach. She had almost the identical expression as Elizabeth Taylor had when she was telling the story of how the desperately poor and starving kids on the beach had devoured Montgomery Clift.

The grilled cheese sandwiches and coconut milkshakes arrived before Roy's mother returned but Roy ignored the food and continued to stare at the girl. The café was in Little Havana, on Southwest 8th Street, close to the dermatologist's office. Roy had been there twice before and he and his mother always ordered the same thing. Everyone in the café, which was named La Cafetería Fabuloso, was speaking Spanish, so Roy assumed the beautiful girl was Cuban, like most of the people in this part of Miami. He wondered why she was alone and imagined she worked in a shop somewhere in the barrio.

His mother came back and said, "Oh, good, I'm starved. Aren't you, Roy? I couldn't get Margie to stop complaining about Ronaldo. I told her to just tell him to go back to his wife."

Roy took a sip of his milkshake through the straw in the glass and thought about those wild boys biting into Monty Clift's flesh. Elizabeth Taylor told the psychiatrist, or Katherine Hepburn, who played Montgomery Clift's mother, Roy couldn't remember who, how there had been nothing she could do to stop them.

"Come on, Roy, we don't have much time."

The girl stood up. She was taller than Roy expected her to be, and slender, not short and buxom like Elizabeth Taylor. She still had a terrified expression on her face, as if she expected something bad to happen to her as soon as she left the café.

"I'm glad it's raining today," said Roy's mother. "Too much sun makes me want to wriggle out of my skin like a snake."

Roy watched the girl walk out. She was wearing a pink cotton dress and did not carry an umbrella. Roy wanted to get up and follow her.

"We're late, Roy. If you're not hungry now, wrap up your sandwich in a napkin and we'll take it with us. You can eat it at the dermatologist's."

VULTURES

"In Africa, some tribes believe that wearing a freshly decapitated vulture head can give a person the ability to see into the future."

Roy was sitting on a bench against a wall in Henry Armstrong's second floor boxing gym in Miami listening to Derondo Simmons, a former middleweight once ranked number five in the world by *Ring* magazine. Derondo was forty-two years old and worked as a sparring partner for up-and-comers. Mostly he hung around Henry's and talked to whoever would listen. He was a great storyteller and a voracious reader, especially in the areas of ancient history and anthropology. Roy, who was nine, was a willing audience for Derondo's lectures, and Derondo appreciated it.

"You're a great listener, Roy," he said. "It will pay off for you in the future."

"Pay off how?"

"If you listen carefully, you can figure out how a person's mind works, how they think, then you know what you've got to do to get them to pay you."

Roy's father often dropped him off at the gym when he had business to do downtown. He'd make a contribution to Armstrong's Retired Fighters Fund and press something into Derondo's hand and know they would keep a close eye on his son until he returned.

"Did you ever have a vulture head?" Roy asked Derondo.

"Only seen 'em in pictures and the movies."

"There's vultures in the Everglades."

"Don't take to snakes and gators, Roy, and I don't want snakes or gators takin' to me. I don't go into the 'glades because I can't figure how those creatures think, or even if they do think. Did you know that in ancient Rome soldiers rode two horses at a time, standing up?"

Henry signaled to Derondo and he got up and went over to the larger of the two rings where Henry was talking to a small, well-dressed man wearing a Panama hat. Standing above them leaning down over the top rope was a lean young guy with boxing gloves on. Roy pegged him as a welterweight in the making, a few pounds shy, sixteen or seventeen years old. Derondo nodded his head while Henry spoke to him, and when Henry stopped talking Derondo walked around to the other side of the ring, slipped a sleeveless sweatshirt over his T-shirt, let one of the ring boys grease his face then wrap his hands before fitting on the gloves and fastening his headgear. The kid in the ring began bouncing around, shadowboxing, getting warm. Derondo climbed through the ropes, did a few deep knee bends, practiced a couple of combinations and uppercuts then motioned to the kid.

Roy went over to ringside and stood near Henry and the man wearing the Panama. Derondo outweighed the boy by twenty-five pounds, so Roy knew he would not throw any hard leather. For the kid's part, it was not unexpected that he would be faster both with his hands and feet. Neither Henry nor the man in the hat, who Roy figured was the boy's manager, said a word for the first minute, then Panama shouted, "No baile! Pégale!"

Roy understood that Panama wanted his boy to prance less and punch more. The kid could not get inside on Derondo, who took whatever the boy offered on his arms and shoulders and did not himself do more than feint and tap. Printed in cursive in gold letters on both sides of the boy's black trunks were the words El Zopo. Suddenly, Derondo threw a left hook off a jab that landed flush on the kid's right temple. The little welter tilted onto his left leg and froze for a moment like a crane or heron in the shallows before toppling over and landing on his left ear. Henry jumped into the ring and he and Derondo bent over him. Panama stayed put while Henry and Derondo helped the boy to his feet.

Roy looked over at Panama and examined his face. He had a thin, dyed black mustache, almond eyes with pale flecks in them and no chin. Roy thought the man resembled a small monkey, a marmoset. When Panama walked around to where Henry and the ring boy were talking to the kid, Roy went back to the bench and leaned against the wall.

A few minutes later, Derondo came and sat down next to him. He had removed the headgear, gloves and sweatshirt and sat still, staring straight ahead for several seconds before saying, "I tell you, Roy, if I'd had a decapitated vulture head I could have told you that kid has no future as a fighter."

Roy's father picked him up an hour later. When they reached the bottom of the forty-seven steps Roy asked him what el zopo means in English.

"Deformed. A deformed person, like in a sideshow. Why?"

"A boxer had it written on his trunks."

"Did he look weird?"

"No, he looked okay. He was just a kid. He was sparring with Derondo Simmons and Derondo knocked him down. I don't think he meant to."

Roy felt safe walking on the street with his father. There were always a few stumblebums on 7th Street outside Henry's; people who had lost their way, his dad called them.

I ALSO DEAL IN FURY

"Then that greaseball actor shows up, and guess who's with him?"

"What actor?"

"Guy with black, curly hair was in the picture where the giggling creep pushes the old lady in a wheelchair down the stairs."

"The actor pushed the woman in the wheelchair?"

"No, the other one, the cop. He's got the rich kid's wife with him, the brunette the queer actor falls for so he drowns his pregnant girlfriend."

"The same movie?"

"No, another one."

"I don't go to the pictures much. I get antsy. Half of the show I'm in the lobby smokin', waitin' on Yvette."

"*I Also Deal in Fury*, you didn't see it?"

"No."

"Anyway, they don't want nobody to know they're in Vegas together, but after ten minutes it's all over town."

"What did they expect?"

"In for the weekend."

"They want privacy they go to the springs, get a mud bath."

Roy was sitting next to the men on a pile of unsold newspapers waiting for his father. It was three-thirty in the morning and his father had said he'd be back at the liquor store by three. Phil Priest and Eddie O'Day were keeping an eye on the boy.

"You okay, kid?" Eddie asked. "Your dad'll be here soon."

"Here," said Phil. "Take it by the grip."

Phil Priest pulled a snubnose .38 out from inside his coat and handed it to Roy.

"You ever handled a piece?"

"Phil, you nuts?" said Eddie. "His old man won't like it, he finds out."

"Be careful, kid," Phil said, "Don't touch the trigger."

"Is it loaded?" Roy asked.

"You got always to assume a piece is loaded. And never point it at anyone other than you mean business."

"It's heavy," said Roy. "Heavier than I thought."

"How old are you now, Roy?"

"Ten. How old are you?"

"Thirty-two."

Roy's father came in and saw Roy holding the gun. Phil took it from him and replaced it inside his coat.

"Roy," said his father, "go stand outside for a minute. By the door, where I can see you."

Roy slid off the stack of newspapers, walked out and stood by the entrance. He liked being up late and looking at people on the street. They were different than the people he saw during the day and in the evening who hung around his father's place. Their faces were hidden even under the lights from the signs on the clubs and restaurants. Phil and Eddie came out of the store and walked away without saying anything.

"Dad, can I come back in now?"

Roy's father came out and stood next to him and draped his right arm around Roy's shoulders. He was wearing a white shirt with the long sleeves rolled up to his elbows and a blue tie with a gold clasp with his initials engraved on it.

"It's cooler out here," he said. "Chicago gets so hot in the summer."

"Are you angry at Phil for showing me his gun?"

A girl came by and stopped and whispered into Roy's father's ear. Her high heels made her taller than his father. She walked around the corner onto Rush Street.

"What did she say, Dad?"

"Thank you."

"For what?"

"I helped her out with something the other day."

"What's her name?"

"Anita."

"She's tall."

"She's a dancer at The Casbah."

"Dad?"

"Yes, son?"

"Are you still angry at Mom?"

"No, Roy. I'm not angry at your mother."

"What about Phil?"

HOUR OF THE WOLF

When he was eleven years old, Roy began waking up between four and four-thirty in the morning, four hours before he had to leave for school. His mother, her husband and Roy's sister were asleep and so long as he kept to the back of the house he did not disturb them. No matter what the weather was, even if it was freezing or raining, Roy liked to go out onto the back porch to feel the fresh air and watch the sky. He could imagine that he lived alone, or at the least that this third stepfather did not exist. Roy had come to understand that his mother gave very little thought to how her bringing these men into his life might affect him. He knew now that it was up to him to control his own existence, to no longer be subject to her poor judgment and desperation.

It was on a morning in mid-December when Roy was standing on the porch wearing a parka over his pajamas looking up at a crescent moon with snow beginning to flurry that he heard a scream. It came from the alley behind his house. Roy could not identify the sound as having come from a woman or a man. He waited on the porch for a second cry but none came. Roy went inside to his room and exchanged his slippers for shoes and went back out. He pulled the hood of his parka over his head and walked carefully down the porch steps, not wanting to slip on the new snow, and continued through the yard along the passageway that led to the alley. Flakes were falling faster, translucent parachutists infiltrating the darkness.

92

Roy looked both ways in the alley but did not see a person. He stood there waiting to hear or see someone or something move. He was about to go back to the house when he saw a shadow creep across the garage door directly opposite his own. Instinctively, he retreated a few steps toward the passageway. The shadow was low and long, as if cast by a four-footed animal, a large dog or a wolf, although he knew there were no wolves in Chicago. What if one, or even a panther, had escaped from a zoo? But could an animal have emitted such a human-like scream? Roy knew that he should go back inside the house but his curiosity outweighed his fear, so he waited, ready to run should a dangerous creature, man or beast, reveal itself.

A car appeared at the entrance to the alley, its headlights burning into the swirling snow. Roy watched the car advance slowly, listening to its tires crunch over the quickly thickening ground cover. As the vehicle came closer, he stepped back further into the passageway, wanting not to be seen by the driver. The car crept past his hiding place and slid to a stop twenty feet away. Roy could not see the car clearly enough to identify the make. Nobody got out. The car sat idling, its windshield wipers whining and thunking.

Roy imagined the driver or perhaps a passenger was looking for the person or animal responsible for the scream. If so, why didn't someone get out of the car and call out or look around? What if the object of their search were injured or frightened, unable to make its distress and location known? After a full minute, the car moved forward, heading toward the far end of the alley. When Roy could no longer see its tail lights, he walked back through the passageway to his house.

His mother's husband was standing on the porch holding a flashlight.

"The back door was open," he said. "What are you doing out there?"

Roy remained at the foot of the porch steps, looking at this man he never wanted to see again. He could feel the snow leaking around the edges of his parka hood, water dripping onto his neck.

"I heard a scream," Roy said.

"You probably had a nightmare. Lock the door after you come in."

The flashlight clicked off and Roy's mother's husband went inside. The snow let up a little but there still was no light in the sky. Roy sat down on the bottom step. It was almost Christmas and he knew that what he wanted was what he didn't want.

LOST MONKEY

Secret Jones cleaned windows in rich people's houses during the day and returned to the houses when he knew the occupants would be away and burglarized them. Secret worked alone and made a steady living. He lived modestly in a small apartment on North Avenue but took a two or three week holiday once a year, usually a luxury cruise to either Caribbean or Mediterranean ports-of-call during the fierce Chicago winters.

Nights he wasn't working, Secret Jones often stopped into Roy's father's liquor store to mingle with other characters who used the store as an unofficial meeting place. Secret was one of the few Negroes among mostly Italian, Irish, Jewish and Eastern European men who hung out at the sandwich counter, seated on stools nursing lukewarm cups of coffee, nibbling stale doughnuts and smoking cigarettes and cigars, or just stood around talking or pretending to be waiting for someone. The liquor store was in the center of the nightclub district and stayed open 24 hours. Roy's father was usually there or in the vicinity from noon until four or five in the morning. Nights when he didn't have school the next day, his father let Roy hang around "to figure out for yourself what bad habits not to pick up."

Secret Jones was one of the men Roy enjoyed listening to.

"You know how I got my name?" Secret said. "My daddy was sixteen and my mama was fifteen when I was born and they

95

wanted to keep me a secret, so that's what my grandmama called me, Mamie June Jones, my mama's mama. She was the one raised me. This was in Mississippi. My daddy bugged out before I could know him and my mama got on the stem and died of alcohol poisoning when I was four years old. How old are you now, Roy?"

"Nine."

"I been on my own since I turned thirteen, after Mamie June passed. I come up to Chi on the midnight special with nothin' but what I was wearin', no laces in my shoes, no belt for my trousers. Thirteen years old stood in Union Station with nothin' in my pockets, that's for real. You're lucky you got a daddy looks out for you. That's what life is about, Roy, or should be, people lookin' out for each other, whether they be blood related or not. Here it is 1956, ninety-one years since President Abraham Lincoln freed my people and there's still places in this country I get shot or strung up I go there. Ain't that a bitch! Same all over, some folks bein' left out or rubbed out and nobody do anything about it."

"Quit cryin', Secret," said Hersch Fishbein. "It ain't only your people catch the short end. How about my six million Hitler done in?"

Hersch, Secret and Roy were sitting at the counter. Hersch worked days at Arlington Park racetrack as a pari-mutuel clerk and sometimes at night at Maywood when the trotters were running.

"You hear about Angelo's monkey?" Hersch asked.

"The organ grinder?" said Secret.

"Angelo's my friend," said Roy. "Dopo sits here at the counter with me and dunks doughnuts in Angelo's coffee."

"Somebody stole him."

"Why would anyone steal Dopo?" Roy asked.

"Sell him," said Secret Jones. "Smart monkey like him. People pay to see him do tricks."

Hersch nodded and said, "A carnival, maybe."

"How'd you hear?" Secret asked.

"Saw Angelo on Diversey, grindin' his box. Had a tin cup on the sidewalk. 'Where's Dopo?' I asked. 'Disappear,' said Angelo. 'I can no passa da cup anna play at same time.'"

"We should look for him," said Roy.

"Hard findin' a little monkey in a city as big as Chicago," Secret said.

Roy went outside where his father was standing on the sidewalk in front of the store talking to Phil Priest, an ex-cop.

"Dad, Hersch says someone stole Dopo, Angelo's monkey."

Phil Priest laughed and said, "A wino probably ate it."

Roy punched Phil on his right arm.

"Take it easy, son," said his father.

"You've got to do something, Dad. Angelo can't make a living without Dopo collecting coins and tipping his hat."

"I'll see what I can do, Roy."

Roy remembered the time he was sitting at the counter doing homework and Angelo and Dopo came in and Dopo picked up a pencil and began imitating Roy, making marks on a piece of paper.

"Dopo helping you," Angelo said.

Roy looked up and down the street. It was ten o'clock at night, not a good time to start hunting for Dopo. Roy would begin the next day asking around the neighborhood if anybody had seen Angelo's monkey, although Angelo had probably already done that.

Phil Priest took off and Roy's father said, "If Dopo doesn't turn up, the organ grinder'll get another monkey."

"I don't like Phil Priest, Dad. Mom says he was a crooked cop, that's why he was kicked off the force. I didn't like what he said about Dopo. It'll take a long time for Angelo to train a new monkey."

Roy walked back inside. Hersch and Secret were arguing about the best way to fix a horse race. Hersch said you had to have the jockeys in your pocket and Secret said it was better to juice the nags.

"None of the bums who hang around your dad's store are on the level," Roy's mother had told him. "Some are worse than others."

"Why does Dad let them stay there?"

"Those men are just part of the system, Roy. Being on the game is all they know, they grew up with it."

"I'm growing up with it, too."

"You won't be like them," said his mother.

Roy's father was still out on the sidewalk, talking to a man Roy had never seen before. The man walked away and Roy went out again.

"Dad?"

"What is it, son?"

"Mom says when I grow up I won't be like the men around here."

Roy's father looked at him and said, "How does she know?"

WHEN BENNY LOST HIS MEANING

Roy was sitting at the counter in the Lake Shore Liquor Store on a Saturday morning in November sipping a vanilla Coke listening to Lucio Stella and Baby Doll Hirsch talk.

"Remember Mean Well Benny?" asked Lucio.

"Worked for Jewish Joe. Spidery little guy. Got rung up for killin' a crooked cop."

"McGuire, in Bridgeport. The Paddy guarded the mayor's house."

"What about him?"

"He's out. Mastro seen him at Murphy's day before yesterday, eatin' a steak without his teeth in."

"What happened to his teeth?"

"Guess he had 'em yanked in prison. Mastro said Benny put his choppers in a glass of water while he gummed the steak."

"He got plans?"

"Probably."

"We should find out."

"How'd he get that tag, anyway?"

"It was Jocko named him Mean Well because too often he did things he wasn't told to do that didn't turn out well."

"Such as?"

"Time he offered Lou Napoli's girl, Ornella, a lift to Lou's crib, only Lou wasn't expectin' her and happened he was entertaining a waitress from Rickett's at the moment. Napoli worked for Jocko and when Lou told him how it had come about Ornella stabbed him and he almost lost a kidney, Jocko said, 'You know, Benny, he means well.' After that, he was Mean Well Benny to everyone in Chicago, even the cops.

"Shootin' McGuire was a mistake, too. He thought it was McGuire had leaned on Jewish Joe, so he threatened him one evening in Noches de San Juan, a PR bar on North Damen. McGuire took offense, busted Benny in the mouth, so Benny parked a pair in the cop's chest. This was after McGuire got thrown off the force."

"Maybe why he got false teeth in the joint."

Roy liked going with his father to his liquor store on Saturday mornings. All kinds of people came in and Roy liked looking at and listening to them, even and especially if they were a little or a lot crazy. A week later, a day before his ninth birthday, Roy heard Lucio Stella tell Baby Doll Hirsch that Mean Well Benny's corpse was found with his throat cut stuffed into a garbage can in an alley in Woodlawn.

"What could he been doin' in that neighborhood?"

"Probably lookin' to do some woolhead a favor he didn't need."

After Lucio Stella and Baby Doll Hirsch left, Roy asked his father if he had known Mean Well Benny.

"He used to come around. Why do you ask?"

"I just heard Mr. Stella tell Mr. Hirsch that Mean Well Benny's body was found in a trash can."

"Some men's lives don't amount to much, son. They get on the wrong road and don't ever get back on the straight and narrow."

The following Saturday morning Roy's father took Lucio Stella and Baby Doll Hirsch aside and said something to them Roy couldn't hear, then they left without finishing their cups of coffee.

"Dad, did you tell Mr. Stella and Mr. Hirsch to leave because of me?"

"I did."

"Are they on the straight and narrow?"

"They don't know what it means."

SICK

A girl's dead body was found on Oak Street beach by a man walking a dog at five o'clock in the morning of March 5th. The body was clothed in only a black raincoat; there was no identification in the pockets. The girl was judged to be in her late teens or very early twenties, the most notable identifying mark being a six-inch scar on the inside of her left calf. She had light brown hair and brown eyes, height five feet four inches, weight one hundred and five. When discovered, the body was coated with a thin layer of ice. Forensics determined that the girl had been dead since approximately seven o'clock the previous evening. Her stomach and abdominal tract contained only particles of food; she had not eaten for at least two days.

Twelve days later, at four p.m. on March 17th, St. Patrick's Day, perhaps the most festive day of the year in Chicago's substantial Irish community in 1958, a forty-eight year old woman named Mary Sullivan, a native of Belfast, Northern Ireland, who had been a resident of Chicago for twenty-two years, filed a missing persons report at the Division Street precinct, claiming that her daughter, Margaret, had not been in contact with her since March 2nd. Margaret, who fit the description of the corpse found on Oak Street beach on the 5th, including the scar on her leg, worked as a waitress at Don the Beachcomber's restaurant—a strange, or perhaps not so strange, coincidence—and had been living with another girl, Lucille Susto, twenty years old, a recent arrival in the city from West Virginia, who also worked as a waitress in a coffee shop in The Loop. When questioned by police, Lucille Susto told them that she had not seen her roommate since the morning of the 4th, before going to work. Her recollection was that Margaret was not scheduled to work at Don the Beachcomber's that night, a fact corroborated by the manager of the restaurant. Mary Sullivan's husband, Desmond, Margaret's father, had been living in Ireland for the past three years and was not presently in contact with either his wife or daughter; Mary did not have a current address for him. At six-thirty on the evening of the 17th, Mary Sullivan identified the body lying in the morgue as that of her daughter, Margaret.

The man who discovered the body was Paddy McLaughlin, a doorman at the nearby Drake Hotel, who had been walking a standard poodle belonging to a resident of the hotel. McLaughlin, whose brother, James, was a sergeant in the Chicago police department, reported his find to the police immediately upon returning to the Drake Hotel with the dog.

"Look, Roy," his mother said to him while they were having breakfast on the morning of March 6th, "Paddy McLaughlin's picture's in the *Trib*."

The McLaughlins were Roy and his mother's next door neighbors; their sons, Johnny, Billy and Jimmy, were Roy's best friends. Roy, who was eleven years old, looked at the photograph of Mr. McLaughlin dressed in his epauleted doorman's uniform, the brim of his military-style hat fixed precisely in the center of his forehead, the tip of his aquiline nose almost touching his long, thin upper lip.

"He found a dead body,"

"I read the article, Roy. He must have had quite a shock."

When Roy saw Johnny that afternoon he asked him what his father had told the family.

"He said there was nothing to tell other than seeing the girl lying on the sand wrapped in a black raincoat and then calling the cops. My Uncle James says if the body's identified my dad'll be called to appear at an inquest, if there is one. I'm thinkin' about goin' down to the beach to search for clues. Want to come with me?"

Johnny was six months older than Roy. He was interested in science and read all about fingerprinting, blood types and various procedures involving detection.

"The police are doing that," said Roy. "What makes you think we can find something they won't?"

"Happens all the time. In the Hardy Boys books they're always solving crimes the cops can't. The other night on *Ned Nye, Private Eye* a kid discovered a foreign coin in a murderer's apartment that could have belonged only to the victim, brought it to Ned, and that cracked the case."

A light snow was falling at eight-thirty the next morning when Jimmy and Roy arrived at Oak Street beach.

"It's freezing out here," Roy said. "The snow's covering up whatever evidence might still be around."

Waves collapsing on the sand sounded like cats knocking over garbage cans in an alley. Lake Michigan was wrinkled gray and black.

"You can't see anything," said Roy. "Not more than a few hundred yards, anyway. No ships in the distance, no planes in the sky. We should go to the Drake and get hot chocolate in the coffee shop."

"My dad doesn't come on duty today until ten," said Johnny. "We'll go over then. The manager's a pal of his so we won't have to pay. Come on, let's see if we can find something."

After forty-five minutes of searching all Roy had found was a broken pencil and a used rubber. After he unearthed the rubber he asked Johnny if he knew if the girl had been raped.

"If she was, it probably didn't happen on the beach in bad weather. She didn't have any clothes on under the coat, so if the killer molested her he did it somewhere else before he dumped the body here."

Johnny found a toothbrush, cigarette butts, one child's size pink mitten and a broken neck chain. He held up the chain for Roy to see and said, "This might be something."

A cop came along and said to them, "What are you boys up to? This is a crime scene."

"It isn't marked off, officer," said Johnny.

"The snow's coverin' up the markers. You lads had best be moving along."

"Do you know Sergeant James McLaughlin?" Johnny asked. "He's my uncle. I'm Johnny McLaughlin."

"Well, when I get home tonight I'll be sure to tell my wife, Kathleen, guess who I encountered on Oak Street beach this mornin' in the sleet and snow but Sergeant James McLaughlin's nephew, Johnny. Go on now, both of you."

"And my father's Paddy McLaughlin, the head doorman at the Drake Hotel. He found the body."

"Next you'll be tellin' me your mother's Rose of Sharon."

In the Drake coffee shop the boys sat at the counter and ordered hot chocolates.

"I think the killer's a rich guy who lives in a fancy apartment around here, on Lake Shore or Marine Drive," said Johnny. "Probably somebody she knew who worked or she met at Don the Beachcomber's. He raped the girl, strangled her—or maybe, if he was a real pervert, strangled her before raping her—then carried the body down in the dead of night."

Johnny and Roy were finishing their hot chocolates when Paddy McLaughlin came into the coffee shop and sat down on the stool next to his son's.

"Top o' the mornin', fellas," he said. "Bobby, the night man, told me you were visiting. May I inquire as to your purpose?"

"We were searching for clues to the murder," said Johnny.

"A cop ran us off the beach," said Roy.

Mr. McLaughlin put two quarters on the counter and stood up.

"I'll be goin' on the job now," he said. "See that you get home safely, detectives. Don't hitchhike, take the bus."

The girl's killer turned out to be a regular customer at Don the Beachcomber's, who, as Johnny figured, lived a few blocks from the beach.

"Johnny got it right," Roy told Jimmy Boyle. "He pegged where the creep met her and where he lived. "Johnny knew it the morning we went to Oak Street to see if we could find a lead."

"Did you find something?"

"No, Johnny just put it together. Maybe he got a feeling from the spot his dad discovered the body."

"I heard on the radio about people who have a special talent to tune in to the sick mind of a killer," said Jimmy, "to identify with him. It's called havin' a sick sense."

Margaret Sullivan's rapist-murderer was a 42 year old bachelor named Leonard Danzig, an architect, who told the judge at a pre-trial hearing that he had been searching for several years for a direct descendant of the sister of Jesus Christ, whom he believed, like her brother, claimed to have been fathered by the Holy Ghost. Danzig said he felt it was his duty to abort what he described as an immoral lineage in order to cease the false prophesies that had wrought chaos since the blasphemy of immaculate conception. Danzig's rationale for the rape was to anneal "the unspeakable insult."

Leonard Danzig did not stand trial but was instead committed for the remainder of his natural life to the Hermione Curzon Institution for the Hopelessly Irreparable in Moab, Illinois.

"Jimmy Boyle's father says Danzig should have gotten the electric chair," Roy told his mother. "What do you think?"

"You can't execute all of the sick people in the world, Roy. There are too many. Once you start doing that it would never stop."

"Don't you think the world would be better off if Leonard Danzig wasn't in it?"

Roy's mother, who had already been divorced twice and had a third marriage annulled, said, "Him and a few other men I can name."

THE BEST PART OF THE STORY

Roy and four other boys, all of them twelve or thirteen years old, were standing in front of Papa Enzo's Pizza Parlor talking and smoking cigarettes, just hanging out even though the temperature outside was well below freezing. A foot of snow had fallen the day before, most of it had hardened and iced over, but the boys, wearing parkas or peacoats, did not mind the cold, they were used to the Chicago winters; only when a fearsome wind was tearing in from the lake did they not gather on the street, especially on weekend nights such as this one. They could hear Buddy Holly's new record "Maybe Baby," coming from the jukebox inside Enzo's.

It was almost ten o'clock when Jimmy Boyle noticed Logo Leberko lurking next to the doorway of Papa Enzo's restaurant.

"Hey, guys, look—there's that creep Leberko standin' by the entrance. I thought he was still locked up at St. Charles."

"Nah," said Tommy Cunningham, "Bobby Dorp told me yesterday they couldn't keep him in the reformatory after he turned eighteen. They either had to release him or transfer him to Joliet."

"He and another guy robbed Koszinski's Bakery, didn't they?" Roy asked.

"Tried to," said Boyle. "It was so stupid. Leberko's mother works there and when he and Dion Bandino stuck up the joint Logo's old lady was behind the counter. Accordin' to the article about it in the *Trib*, Leberko said, 'Ma, I thought you weren't

107

workin' today,' and she said she was fillin' in for someone who was out sick, so she identified him for the cops."

"That's crazy," said Roy. "They really went through with the robbery even though his mother was there?"

"That's the best part of the story," said Richie Gates. "They had guns, my brother told me. He used to deliver cakes for Koszinski's, so he heard all about it. Both Leberko and Bandino had 'em in their hands when they went in."

"Did Bandino get sent to St. Charles, too?" asked Roy.

"Yeah," said Cunningham, "but he got out sooner 'cause he was only fifteen."

"Leberko's a moron," Jimmy said. "Remember how he was always shakin' down younger kids for their milk money at Clinton? He'd take their change then stomp on the kids' lunchboxes and slap 'em around even though they'd already come across."

"He got me once," said Richie. "After that I took off if I saw him in the schoolyard. He didn't get past fourth grade, then they had to let him out when he turned sixteen."

"His old man was murdered in prison," said Tommy Cunningham. "Other inmates set him on fire in his cell."

"No shit," Jimmy Boyle said.

"Yeah. My father thinks he was snitchin' for the guards."

The door of Papa Enzo's opened and two people came out, one of whom was Dion Bandino. Leberko came up quickly behind him and with an eight inch switchblade cut Bandino's throat clear across. Blood exploded out of Bandino's neck like flames being tossed out of a bucket, turning the snow at his feet into a sea of vermilion. For what seemed to Roy a long time, though it was only a few seconds, nobody moved except Leberko, who disappeared. Dion Bandino was dead and didn't know it as his body accordioned down and knelt with his chin resting on his chest.

Roy and Jimmy Boyle took off in one direction and Richie Gates and Tommy Cunningham in another without looking back.

After they'd run as fast as they could for a few blocks, Jimmy and Roy stopped to catch their breath, and Jimmy said, "I thought Bandino would fall forward. He just dropped and didn't topple over."

"I never saw anybody get their throat slit before."

"We can't say nothin' about it, Roy. Don't tell nobody we were there. We don't want the cops to make us be witnesses against Leberko. If somehow he beat the rap he'd come after us like he done Bandino."

"Why do you think he did it?"

"Bandido must've caved, maybe said the stick-up was Logo's idea, that he'd been forced into it by an older guy."

Roy was still gasping for air; even in the darkness he could see his breath.

"I'm goin' home," he said.

"Me, too," said Jimmy. "Remember, don't tell anyone we were there."

When he got home, Roy's mother was sitting alone at the kitchen table. Her eyes were red and her face was swollen.

"Hi, Ma, why're you cryin'? Are you all right?"

"Not really, no, Roy, but it's nothing you have to worry about. Did you have a good time with the boys?"

"It's too cold to be outside."

"I'm going to make a pot of tea. Do you want some?"

"No, thanks. I'm pretty tired. I'm going to lie down in my room. Are you sure you're okay?"

"Yes, Roy. It's just that Dan and I have decided to not see each other any more. It's for the best, I know, we're really not a good match, but I feel like my dog just died."

"We've never had a dog."

"Oh, you must know what I mean. It's not the end of the world, but it's a kind of death, nevertheless. There are all kinds of deaths. Some stay with you more than others, you'll see."

Four days later the police found Logo Leberko hiding in the boiler room of an apartment building a few blocks away from Papa Enzo's Pizza Parlor; scraps of food he'd scavenged from garbage cans were scattered on the floor and he was covered with rat bites. Roy and his friends were not questioned about the incident; other witnesses, including Dion Bandino's companion that night, Arvid Gustafsson, whose mother also worked at Koszinski's Bakery and was the person Leberko's mother was substituting for the day of the robbery, fingered Logo as the killer.

On their way to school one day the next week Richie Gates told Roy that his brother was delivering cakes again for Koszinski's.

"Is Leberko's mother still working there?"

"Yeah. Floyd heard her tellin' a customer that Logo'll get the chair unless he gets whacked in stir first, like his father. She says her son is already dead to her and it's like he never even existed. Think she means it or she's just sayin' that to make herself not feel bad?"

"Both, maybe," said Roy.

"I'm sure if somethin' happened to me," Richie said, "my mother wouldn't try to convince herself I'd never been alive. What about yours?"

TELL HIM I'M DANGEROUS

Roy came home from work at the Red Hot Ranch around ten-thirty and found his mother sitting alone on the couch in the livingroom watching TV. He was fifteen years old and his mother was thirty-eight. She had recently been divorced from her third husband, by whom she had a child, Roy's sister, Sally, who was almost four.

"Hi, Ma, Sally asleep?"

"Yes, Roy, just now. I let her stay up late. I was teaching her how to play gin rummy. She caught on fast."

"That doesn't surprise me, Sally's smart."

"I was smart once, too," said his mother. "How was work?"

"All right. Busy, like every Saturday. I thought you were going out tonight with Kay and Harvey."

"They wanted me to meet a friend of theirs, a guy who's in town from Minneapolis, to show him Chicago. A business associate of Harvey's. Made a lot of money in jukeboxes, Kay told me. But I'm not up to it. Besides, Madeleine couldn't babysit tonight, she's got a date."

"She's a cute girl," said Roy, "lots of boys like her. She's sixteen. I think her babysitting days are over."

"Madeleine's a nice kid, I hope she makes good choices. I'm off men for now."

"I'm a man."

"You're my son, my beautiful boy. Come sit and watch a movie with me. It's just about to come on. I saw it when it came out, in 1948, just before you were born. Roxanne Hudnut and Diane Root as sisters."

"One good, one bad?"

"Both kind of bad, if I remember right. One more than the other."

"Okay, Ma, I'll wash up a little first."

The movie's title was *Tell Him I'm Dangerous*. Roxanne Hudnut and Dianne Root were still in their twenties when it was made, as had been Roy's mother when she'd seen it in a theater. She always identified with Roxanne Hudnut, whom she resembled. Both of them were brunettes with slightly slanted chestnut eyes that gave their faces an almost oriental look. When they looked up at you slowly or sideways it was easy to believe they were keeping dark secrets. *Tell Him I'm Dangerous* was in black and white, as were most of Roxanne Hudnut and Diane Root's movies, many of which were mysteries of some kind involving crimes of passion. Roy sat down on the couch half way through the opening credits. His mother had a blanket over her legs.

"Tell me if you get chilly, Roy," she said. You can share the blanket."

The time of the movie was present day late 1940s. A young woman named Ann Rivers, played by Roxanne Hudnut, arrives in a small midwestern town, asks for and gets a job in a flower shop run by an older woman, Mrs. Morgan. Ann tells her that she's recently dropped out of business college, secretarial school, in the capital city. She needs a break from that hectic life. Ann says she has no immediate family, that both of her parents are dead and she has no siblings. Mrs. Morgan is a kind lady and helps her find a room to rent in a local boarding house with a good reputation run by Mr. and Mrs. Drummond, a middleaged couple.

At the Drummond house Ann meets another resident, Lee Lockwood, a contractor and structural engineer, who is in town working on the repair of a bridge. He's a few years older than Ann, calm with a pleasant manner.

"He looks a little like Dick Brothers, only shorter. Remember him, Roy? That car dealer I had a few dates with?"

A few days after their first meeting, Lee Lockwood invites Ann out to dinner. They begin spending time together but she avoids giving him any detailed information about her background other than what she's told Mrs. Morgan. Three weeks later another young woman arrives in the town, also a stranger, and tells people that she's searching for her younger sister, Ann Rivers. Her name is Sarah Rivers. Sarah is directed to Mrs. Morgan's flower shop, where she introduces herself to Mrs. Morgan. Ann enters and does not seem surprised to find her sister there. Mrs. Morgan is surprised because Ann has told her she had no family. Sarah explains that she and Ann had a falling out and Ann left home, that's all, but Mrs. Morgan remains suspicious, as if there is something left unexplained.

Sarah also rents a room at the Drummond house, where she encounters Lee Lockwood, to whom she introduces herself as Ann's slightly older sister. The sisters argue in Sarah's room. Ann had accused Sarah's fiancé, Bob Dean, of attempting to rape her. He was found guilty of sexual assault and sentenced to six months in prison. Sarah has never believed this accusation. Bob Dean denied it, but Ann has stuck to her story.

Ann abruptly stops seeing Lee Lockwood without giving him a reason. He's puzzled but doesn't demand an explanation; after all, he doesn't really know her very well. He becomes friendly with Sarah, who finds a job as a ticket taker in the box office of the local movie theater, the only one in town. Sarah tells Ann that Lee has asked her about Ann's refusal to go out with him any more, to which Ann replies, "Tell him I'm dangerous," that he's better off not seeing her.

Lee is a straight shooter, well-liked in the community, doing a good job on the bridge. He and Sarah begin going around together, then become intimate. One night he comes back to his room and finds Ann there, she's been waiting for him. Ann tells Lee that the only reason Sarah is pretending to be interested in him is out of jealousy, that Sarah wants to cause her trouble because of what happened with Bob Dean. She tells Lee about Bob Dean trying to rape her, that Sarah claimed Ann was lying. This is why Ann left home, to escape the controversy and the gossip. "I stopped going out with you because I knew Sarah would try to poison our relationship," Ann says. She then seduces Lee.

"Do you think I look like her, Roy?" asked his mother. "People used to compare me to Roxanne Hudnut all the time."

"Your hair is the same color," Roy said. "Her eyes always seem a little out of focus. When she's supposed to be looking at someone her eyes are staring in a different direction."

Lee Lockwood is mixed up, vulnerable to both sisters. A few days after Ann seduces Lee, Sarah is found dead, hanging in the early morning from the bridge Lee is repairing. People initially assume it was suicide, but then Ann accuses Lee of murdering Sarah because she was pregnant with Lee's child. Lee admits he has been sleeping with Sarah but swears he didn't kill her. Lee is arrested. At his trial Ann tearfully testifies that Sarah told her she was afraid of Lee, of what he might do since Sarah has told him of the pregnancy. She tells the court that she went to see Lee and that he raped her. He denies both charges of murder and rape, and says that Ann formerly accused Sarah's fiancé of attempting to rape her. The prosecuting attorney declares that information to be

114

irrelevant to this case and forces Lee to admit that he made love to Ann when she came to see him about Sarah. Lee is sentenced to life in prison for the murder of Sarah Rivers.

"I told you one sister was worse than the other," said Roy's mother.

"Sarah wasn't good, either. Maybe she was trying to set Lee up," said Roy, "that she was really pregnant by Bob Dean."

"That's good, Roy. I didn't think of that."

Soon after the trial, Ann is found dead hanging from the bridge. A crowd has gathered to watch the removal of her body by the police, which is shown through the point of view of a man among the spectators. After Ann's body is loaded into an ambulance and driven away, the man walks to a car and begins driving. As he drives, the movie flashes back through his mind, reliving the sequence of events that have led up to Ann's death: Ann seducing this man, whom we now realize is Bob Dean, then accusing him of attempted rape; his being confronted by Sarah after Ann tells her that Bob attacked her; Bob's contention that Ann acted out of jealousy over Sarah's relationship with him; and finally Bob is shown appearing in Ann's room at the boarding house and forcing her to write a letter confessing that she killed Sarah and hung her from the bridge, which is also shown in flashback as Ann writes.

The movie switches back to present time as Mrs. Morgan is opening a letter in her flower shop. It's the confession Bob Dean forced Ann to write. Also enclosed in the envelope is a second letter, written by Bob. Both letters are heard in voice over by Ann and Bob as Mrs. Morgan reads them. In Bob's letter he admits that Sarah was in fact carrying his child and that he killed Ann and hung her body from the bridge. The final two shots in present time are of Bob Dean driving away into the distance and Lee Lockwood being released from prison.

Then comes a surprise, a coda in which two little girls, each about four years old, are sitting next to each other on chairs playing with dolls. One girl says to the other, "I couldn't sleep last night." Girl number two says, "What did you do?" Girl number one answers, "I woke up my sister." "Why?" asks girl number two. "If I can't sleep, she shouldn't either," says girl number one. Girl number two asks, "Do you like your sister?" "I hate her!" answers girl number one, who then tears her doll apart.

Roy got up from the couch and turned off the sound on the television as the end credits rolled, then sat back down.

"Do you think that was a good idea to have a scene with those two little girls?" asked his mother.

"Sure, it's so you know that Ann was jealous of Sarah from the beginning. Ann was more evil than her sister."

"Do you really think Sarah was evil?"

"Yes, like I said, she stole Lee Lockwood away from Ann and wanted him to believe that he was the father of her unborn child."

"But Ann had stopped seeing him."

"I think she was still keeping him on the hook, to make him uncertain of how she felt, to control him."

"Roxanne Hudnut played bad good," said Roy's mother. "When they put her in more sympathetic roles she was never completely believable, especially musicals. She couldn't dance."

"Why did she stop making movies?" Roy asked.

"She got involved with the actor who played Bob Dean, Mark Brown. She married him. They had a couple of kids, then she had a nervous breakdown, maybe even tried to commit suicide, and was in and out of mental hospitals for years."

"Is she still alive?"

"I think so. Brown divorced her. It's a rotten business, the movies. A girl gets old, you're no use to them. The producers need fresh faces. Beauty sells. Once it fades a girl gets desperate."

"There are parts for older women."

His mother threw off the blanket and stood up.

"It's not the same, Roy. A pretty girl gets used to the way the world looks at her. Not just men, women, too. Roxanne Hudnut wasn't prepared for life after she changed, and she probably didn't have any help, the right kind of help. I guess the same thing happens to everyone. Good night, sweetheart, I'm going to bed. Thanks for staying up with me."

Roy stared at the TV with the sound off for a few minutes before he got up and turned it off. He knew his mother thought of herself as being a little like Roxanne Hudnut, even though she hadn't been a movie star, as if she didn't have much to look forward to, even the lives of her children. Roy was old enough now to know there was nothing he would ever be able to do about it.

THE SHADOW GOING FORWARD

Roy's father never spoke to him about his illness. Roy was ten when he first noticed that anything was wrong. Since his parents were divorced and he lived with his mother Roy did not even know that his father had been in the hospital let alone had surgery. It was not until he was at his father's house a month or more after the surgery that Roy saw his father sitting on a round rubber pillow at his kitchen table.

"How come you're sitting on that pillow, Dad?" Roy asked.

"Well, son, when somebody gives me a pain in the ass this makes me feel better."

"Was it Moe Jaffe? You always say he's a pain in the ass. Like the time he went to the track before depositing the receipts in the bank and dropped everything on a longshot named Remy's Desire?"

"Not this time."

"Does it hurt?"

"Only when I think about my trusting Moe or some other vecchio rimbambito to do something."

"Jimmy Boyle couldn't sit at his desk in school for two days after Angelo's monkey Dopo bit him on the ass."

"Why did Dopo bite him?"

"He saw Jimmy snatch a doughnut from Angelo's stand and start eating it without paying for it first."

His father gave a little laugh but Roy could see him grimace whenever he moved, so he didn't ask him about it again.

A few months later Roy's father began spending more and more of his time at home in bed and didn't want to have any visitors, even Roy.

"He needs to rest, Roy," his father's second wife, Ellie, told him. "You can see him when he feels better. I'll let you know when it's a good time."

Roy liked Ellie and trusted her, so he waited, but before he was allowed to go over to his father's house again Roy's mother told him he was dead.

"Your dad fought hard," his mother said, "you know how tough he was, and the doctors did everything they could for him."

Roy's father was only forty-eight when he died. Too young to die, Roy heard a dozen or more people say at the wake. Moe Jaffe was there, and he draped his long right arm around Roy's shoulders. Roy looked up at Moe's nose, which also was very long and dotted with pockmarks; the tip of it hung over his upper lip. Everything about Moe was long, even the lobes of his ears reached to his shirt collar.

"God must've needed him," Moe said to Roy. "He must need your father to help straighten somethin' out, somethin' he can't fix all by Himself. Trust me, Roy, Rudy'll be the man for the job. You can be sure of that."

"Do you know what a vecchio rimbambito is?" Roy asked him.

The deep wrinkles in Moe Jaffe's forehead tangled together like vines in the Amazon jungle and his eyes crossed and uncrossed before he said, "No, Roy, I don't. What is it?"

"My dad's not one, so maybe you're right."

Moe removed his arm from Roy's shoulders and Roy walked away, past his mother and Ellie, who were talking to one another, past a bunch of people he didn't know who were eating pastries and drinking wine and whiskey, and out of what had been his father's house. It was hot outside, so Roy took off his sportcoat, dropped it on the ground next to the front door and walked down the street.

Some older boys were playing baseball in the park at the end of the block. Roy sat down on the grass next to the field and watched them. God didn't need his father, he thought. The kid playing shortstop kept booting ground balls. He didn't have soft hands. One thing Roy knew for sure was that if you want to play short-stop you have to have soft hands.

Years later, when Roy was in Rome, he asked an older Italian man, a writer, what "vecchio rimbambito" meant. The man raised an eyebrow, laughed briefly, and said, "That's a very old world expression, Roy. It means old fool or dotard, someone who behaves in a childish manner, perhaps due to senility. Where did you hear it?"

"When I was a boy my father used those words to describe someone who worked for him, a person who sometimes acted foolishly."

"You grew up in Chicago, didn't you?"

"Yes, I was born there, but my father didn't go to live in America until he was ten years old."

"It's the kind of description you could still hear in Napoli or Reggio Calabria, more-likely in Sicily. Yes, it's Siciliano, a term an elderly mafioso might use. What was your father's family's business in Chicago?"

FEELING THE HEAT

Standing outside in the oppressive heat and humidity of Miami at eleven o'clock in the morning was not what Roy's mother expected. She and Roy, who was five years old, were waiting in a long line to enter a theater in order to attend a free advance screening of the new Hopalong Cassidy movie and have an opportunity to obtain the autograph of William Boyd, the actor who had portrayed "Hoppy", as the cowboy hero was familiarly known, in movies and in a television series for more than twenty years. William Boyd had been a leading man in silent films and early talkies before taking on the black-clad character of an Old West crime fighter. Boyd had been a matinee idol in his youth, was renowned as a ladies man, and now, in his fifties, he sported a full head of wavy, snow-white hair that crowned a still-handsome face.

"I don't know how much longer I can take this," Roy's mother said to him. "There's no shade and no place to sit down. I know how much you like Hoppy, Roy, but maybe we just ought to wait and see the movie when it opens."

This was in 1952, when westerns were very popular. Most of the kids waiting in the hot sun were dressed like Hopalong Cassidy, wearing stovepipe-high black cowboy hats, black shirts and pants, with a white bandanna tied around their neck and double holster gunbelts housing a pair of white-handled cap pistols.

"But Mom, Hoppy's here!" Roy said. "I want him to sign his name on my hatband."

Before Roy's mother could complain again, many of the kids began shouting and pointing.

"Look!" cried Roy. "There he is! It's Hoppy!"

William Boyd, dressed in full Hopalong Cassidy regalia, was walking slowly along the line, shaking hands with the kids, nodding politely and tipping his hat to their parents. When he got to Roy and his mother, the actor stopped and looked her over carefully. Kitty was in her mid-twenties and still as attractive as she was only a few years before when she had been chosen the University of Texas beauty queen.

"Is this your son?" William Boyd asked her.

"Yes, his name is Roy. He's a great admirer of yours."

"Of Hopalong Cassidy's, you mean," said Boyd. "Howdy, Roy. And, if I may ask, what is your name Roy's mother?"

"Kitty."

William Boyd smiled and took off his hat. Even though there was no breeze, it seemed as if his long white hair were blowing in one. His teeth were sparkling white and even.

"It's extremely hot standing out here, Mr. Boyd. I don't think Roy can take the sun much longer. I know I can't."

"Come with me, Kitty, and Roy. I should be getting back inside anyway."

Roy and his mother stepped out of line and accompanied Hopalong Cassidy to the theater entrance.

Once they were inside, Roy's mother said, "Oh, thank God, it's air-conditioned."

The night before, Kitty had told her friend Kay on the phone that she had decided to leave her husband, Roy's father, who was in Havana, Cuba, doing business with the Morabito brothers, both of whose wives Kitty disliked. She would send her husband a telegram this afternoon, then take the phone off the hook. It would be nice to live someplace that was cooler, Kitty thought, like San Francisco. She and Roy's father had gone there on their honeymoon. Nights were windy, she could wear her fur coat and not have to pin up her hair every day to keep the back of her neck from sweating.

"I'd like to send Roy a few souvenirs, Kitty," said William Boyd. "Where can I reach you?"

A young woman wearing a red-satin cowgirl blouse with a yellow bandanna tied around her neck came over and stood next to him. She was smiling brightly and holding a clipboard and a pen.

"Penny here will take down your contact information," Boyd said. "I have to go backstage now to get ready for the show. It's been swell meeting you, Roy."

The actor reached down and shook Roy's right hand.

"And a pleasure to have met you, Kitty."

"Thank you for rescuing us, Mr. Boyd," she said.

"Bill, you can call me Bill. I'll be in touch."

"Hoppy, could you sign my hat?" Roy asked.

"Please," said Kitty.

"Please," said Roy.

William Boyd replaced his tall black hat on his head. Penny handed him her pen, he signed Roy's hatband, gave the pen back to Penny, tipped his hat to Kitty and walked away.

Roy's mother gave Penny the telephone number of the Delmonico Hotel, where they were temporarily living, she explained, and Penny thanked her, then hurried after the actor.

"Do you think he'll really send me something, Mom?"

"He said he would, Roy. Yes, I believe we'll be hearing from Mr. Boyd."

"He said to call him Bill, remember?"

The other kids and their parents began filing into the theater.

"Come on, Mom, we've got to get seats."

"Oh, Roy, I don't think I'm up to it. The sun really took a lot out of me. We'll see the movie another time. Soon, I promise."

Kitty took Roy's hand and they fought their way through the crowd until they were back outside on the sidewalk.

"Don't be sad, darling," Kitty said, "you got to meet Hoppy personally and he signed your hat. He even knows your name."

"He knows yours, too."

"Uh huh. I could go for a cold milkshake, couldn't you?"

THE SHARKS

Roy was eight years old when he flew with his mother and her boyfriend Johnny Salvavidas from Miami to the Bahamas for a long weekend. There was a casino in the hotel on the island where they stayed and Johnny liked to gamble. During the day, Roy and his mother went to the beach or hung out at the hotel swimming pool while he played blackjack. At night, after dinner, Roy watched TV in their room and Johnny played roulette while Roy's mother watched him lose.

"The wheel is best challenged in the night time," he told Roy. "It's a game that requires witnesses."

"Why?" Roy asked.

"To play boldly, with daring, a man must be brave, and bravery demands an audience. Alone every man is a coward. The ability to conquer one's fears is enhanced by the arousal of blood in others."

"It takes skill, too," said Roy. "My Uncle Buck says to win consistently you have to do the math, that you can't succeed unless you know the odds. He says at roulette the odds are always against you, especially when the wheel has a double zero."

"Johnny knows what he's doing, Roy," said his mother.

The third day they were there the three of them had lunch together on a terrace of the hotel. Both Roy's mother and Johnny Salvavidas were sipping from big glasses with tropical fruits impaled on the rims. Roy was nibbling giant prawns that he dipped into a spicy red sauce. The pieces of chipped ice in the bowl under the prawns melted faster than he could eat them.

"Bob Donovan invited us to go with him and some other guests this afternoon to a beach on the other side of the island," Roy's mother said. "It's supposed to be very beautiful and uncrowded."

"I'm sure it will be," said Johnny.

Johnny Salvavidas was from the Dominican Republic, which was on an island Roy had never been to. His mother had been there once with Johnny. When she came back from that trip to get Roy, whom she had left with his grandmother Rose in Chicago, he overheard his mother telling Rose that in the capital city of Santo Domingo everyone is a thief.

"Johnny told me to never carry any money except for a few coins and not to wear my rings if I went out by myself. He always carried a pistol while we were there."

"Surely not everyone in Santo Domingo is a thief," Rose said. "People work in the sugar mills and the cane fields. Besides, Johnny carries a gun when he's in Chicago, too."

"How do you know that?"

"He told me. He probably thinks everyone in Chicago is a thief."

Roy and his mother accompanied Bob Donovan, who was from Cleveland but had been living in the Bahamas for a few years, and six other hotel guests to Emerald Beach. Bob Donovan drove them in a rusty, blue Chevy van and told them on the way that there was a good restaurant at the beach with a bar in case anyone got hungry or thirsty. The trip took forty minutes over a rough road. Roy's mother asked Bob Donovan what business he'd been in in Cleveland and he said, "Cement. You can't go wrong in cement."

Emerald Beach looked like both of the other beaches Roy and

his mother had already been to but it was uncrowded. In fact, no other swimmers or even sun bathers were there. Roy and his mother went into the water right away. It was crystal clear, like all of the water around the island, and shallow for a long way out. A couple of other people went swimming, too; the rest of the group went to the bar with Bob Donovan and did not go into the water at all during the two or three hours they were there.

When they got back to the hotel, Roy and his mother took showers and then lay down on their beds. Roy fell asleep but woke up when he heard Johnny and his mother talking in loud voices.

"How was I supposed to know it was dangerous?" she said. "You could have warned me."

"Donovan takes tourists there because he gets a kickback from the bar. Nick Turco told me Emerald Beach is shark-infested. That's why no locals go there."

"Who's Nick Turco?"

"A guy I know from Fort Lauderdale. I ran into him in the casino. He's in the construction business. He's down here on a gambling junket."

"You're supposed to take care of us, Johnny. You could have come and taken us back."

She sat down on Roy's bed and held him close to her. Her skin was soft and hot. She was slim with large breasts, long legs and flaming chestnut-colored hair. Roy was beginning to understand why men were attracted to her.

Johnny Salvavidas stood and patted his thick, black mustache with the fingers of his right hand as if it were the top of a dog's head, then he left the room. He said something in Spanish when he was outside in the hallway.

"We're lucky no sharks were at Emerald Beach today, aren't we, Roy?"

"I read in a book about sea creatures that a moray eel has an even stronger bite than a shark's," Roy said. "After it's sunk its teeth in, a moray never lets go. To kill it you have to cut off the head with a machete."

The early evening sun was streaming into the room. Roy's mother got up and drew the curtains.

"Johnny shouldn't be upset," said Roy. "He wasn't the one who could have been bitten by sharks."

SMART GUYS

"The girl used to dance at La Paloma. Jasmine Ford. I don't know if that was her real name."

"It wasn't. Not her first name, anyway. Marlene, Marla, something like that. You thinkin' what?"

"Where's she's got to, that's all."

"You ready to do something dumb again, huh?"

"I'm not a smart guy like you, Freddie."

Harry Castor walked toward LaSalle. He had a room there, a basement. A real comedown, he thought, every time he woke up there or came back to it. No place to bring Jasmine Ford. Castor came from Kansas City, Kansas. He was a musician, a drummer. In Chicago he jammed with guys he met hanging around the clubs, sat in here and there when the opportunity arose. Harry was getting in until he got shot one night in a currency exchange where he'd gone to cash a check from one of his rare gigs. A teenager was killed trading gunfire with a security guard and Castor got caught in the crossfire, taking a slug from the punk in his left hand. The bullet passed through the palm and put a permanent crimp in his career as a percussionist.

After he recovered from the gunshot wound, Harry partnered with Freddie DiMartini selling phony home burglary insurance policies. Roy's friend Jimmy Boyle's uncle, Donal Liffey, had done time at Joliet with DiMartini; according to Jimmy, Liffey was the mastermind behind the insurance scam.

"Uncle Donal says this hustle is foolproof," Jimmy told Roy. "He has his own guys rob an insured house once in a while and he pays off. Those homeowners tell their friends about the Midnight Insurance Company and they sign up, too. It's just him and DiMartini and a new guy, Harry Castor, used to be a jazz drummer. I like Harry. He has a hole in the palm of his left hand he keeps a hundred dollar bill in."

Roy and Jimmy were in the same fifth grade class. They were walking to school together when Jimmy told Roy about his uncle's operation.

"What do you mean he keeps a C-note in a hole in his hand? How'd he get the hole there?"

"Some yom was tryna stick up a currency exchange and Harry walked in on it. The guard draws on the yom, they go high noon, and Harry takes one in the hand."

"Who shot him, the stick-up man or the security guard?"

"I don't know, and neither does Harry. I asked him and he said the slug went out the other side. Could've been from either gun."

A couple of months after Jimmy Boyle told Roy about the scam, the two boys were sitting in the kitchen in Jimmy's house after school eating liver sausage sandwiches when his Uncle Donal came in with Freddie DiMartini and Harry Castor. Donal Liffey, Jimmy's mother's brother, lived with them. He had supported his sister and her son since Jimmy's father was run down and killed walking home at one A.M. from Milt's Tap Room on Elston Avenue two years before. The driver kept going and there were no eyewitnesses. Donal, a bachelor, moved in a few days later and had become the most significant male figure in his nephew's life. Jimmy thought his Uncle Donal was the smartest man in Chicago.

"Hey there, me bucko," Donal said to Jimmy. "Who's your pal?"

Donal was a small but well-built man with thick black hair and squinty blue eyes. He'd been a pretty good amateur lightweight in his youth, and at forty-two he maintained his fighting weight. Donal idolized James Cagney, the way he'd been in *City for Conquest*, where he played a boxer who gets blinded by an opponent's unscrupulous corner men. "All the pros thought Cagney had been a boxer," Donal liked to tell people, "but he hadn't. He was a good dancer and knew how to move, he had the footwork. He spoke Irish and Yiddish, too. Did you know that?"

Freddie DiMartini was only slightly bigger than Donal but he leaned to his right both when he walked or stood still. He said it was because when he was a kid a horse pulling an ice wagon had kicked him in his back, but Donal knew Freddie had taken a beating in reform school that partially crippled him. A guy who'd been in reform school with Freddie told Donal that DiMartini had been stealing the other boys' comic books and they had ganged up on him.

Harry Castor was a large man with big shoulders and big hands, one of which had a hole in it.

"Harry," said Jimmy, "Roy wants to see the Benjamin."

"Harry walked over to where Roy was sitting and held out his left hand, palm open. There was a corner of a bill that had been folded over a few times with the number 100 showing.

"Your dad owns Lake Shore Liquors, doesn't he?" Donal asked Roy.

"Yes," Roy said.

"He's a stand up guy. His name's Rudy, right?"

Roy nodded.

"He did me a good turn once. You got good taste in friends, Jimmy."

Donal shook Roy's hand and then the three men went into a back room and closed the door.

"Does your mom work?" Roy asked Jimmy.

"At Woolworth's on Minnetonka. She's the head of the sewing counter. Uncle Donal tells her she should quit but she likes doin' it. She has friends there she says she'd miss if she didn't see 'em every day. Uncle Donal pays the bills but my mother says what if somethin' happens to him like happened to my father?"

Six weeks later something did happen to Jimmy's Uncle Donal and to Freddie DiMartini, too. They were shotgunned by a man whose house they were breaking into at three o'clock in the morning. Donal was killed and DiMartini was blinded.

"What about Harry?" Roy asked Jimmy Boyle.

"He split," Jimmy said. "He was probably there, maybe drivin' the car, but nobody saw him. My mother got a letter yesterday and the only thing in the envelope was a folded-up hundred dollar bill."

APACHERIA

Roy and his friend Jimmy Boyle were walking to school on a rainy morning when a car passed them going too fast and went out of control, skidding on its two right side wheels before crashing into a telephone pole. The woman who had been driving was thrown from the car and was lying in the street. Roy and Jimmy ran over to see if she was all right. She was on her back with her eyes closed and her mouth open but she was not bleeding. The driver was young, in her late teens or early twenties, and her dress was up around her waist exposing her bare legs and underwear. A few cars passed by without stopping.

"We should call an ambulance," said Jimmy.

A man wearing denim overalls came out of an apartment building and looked at the girl.

"I heard noise," he said. "I'm janitor here."

"Call an ambulance," said Roy.

"I call cops, too."

The man went back into the building. The girl was not moving. She had fluffy, medium-length brown hair, high cheekbones, a short, straight nose and full red lips.

"She's really pretty," Roy said.

"You think we should pull down her dress?" asked Jimmy. "Cover her up?"

"Probably better not to touch her before the ambulance comes."

"Think she's dead?"

"She's breathing. See? Her chest is going up and down."

Rain was still falling lightly when two police cars arrived, followed a few seconds later by an ambulance. By this time a few passersby and residents of nearby houses were gathered on the sidewalk.

"Anybody see how this happened?" asked one of the cops.

"We did," said Jimmy Boyle. "Roy and I were walkin' to school and we seen the car skid and smash into the pole. It's a '56 Chevy."

"Were there other cars on the road? Maybe coming toward her?"

"No," said Roy, "just this one."

He and Jimmy watched as the ambulance attendants tucked a blanket around the unconscious girl from the neck down and lifted her onto a gurney then loaded it into the wagon.

"She have any passengers?" the cop asked. "Anybody walk away from the vehicle after the collision?"

Both Roy and Jimmy shook their heads.

The janitor, who had come back out and was standing next to the boys, said, "I call ambulance. Nobody run."

A tow truck arrived and one of the cops told the spectators to move away from the wrecked car. The ambulance drove off, its siren blaring.

"Okay, boys," said the cop who'd been asking questions, "you'd better go on to school."

Another cop came over and said, "Let's go, Lou. Eisenhower'll be at the Palmer House quarter to ten."

"We're late," Jimmy said to the first cop. "Can you give us a note?"

He removed from one of his pockets a pad of traffic tickets, scribbled on it, ripped out the page and handed it to Jimmy.

"When you boys are old enough to drive remember not to speed on a wet street."

Roy and Jimmy watched the tow truck guys attach cables to the car and signal to the winch operator to pull the car right side up. After that was done they hooked up the front bumper and hauled it away. The cops got back into their cars and headed for The Loop.

"I didn't know the president was comin' to Chicago today," said Jimmy.

"What did the cop write?" Roy asked him.

Jimmy showed the yellow ticket page to Roy, who read it out loud.

"These two boys witnessed a traffic accident this A.M. Car hit pole corner Granville and Washtenaw approx. 8:45. Please excuse them being late. Ofc. P. Madigan, Badge 882."

"Look at this," said Jimmy.

Lying next to the curb where the car had been on its side was a pink make-up compact with a cracked cover. Jimmy picked it up.

"Maybe she was puttin' on make-up while she drove," he said, and put the compact into his right jacket pocket.

"You gonna keep it?"

"Yeah. If the cops come back to inspect the scene I don't want her to get in trouble."

The janitor and the other observers had all gone back into their houses and the boys began walking toward the school.

"You're right," Jimmy said.

"About what?"

"She was pretty. Her legs and everything."

"I felt bad," said Roy, "lookin' at her that way. Part naked, I mean. I hope her neck's not broken."

"Me, too. I couldn't stop lookin' either."

That afternoon in American History Roy was reading about the war with the Apache Indians on the U.S.-Mexico border in the 1870s when he thought about the girl. He wondered if Apaches came across a white woman lying alone and unconscious on a desert trail, maybe thrown from a horse, would they have stopped to help her or leave her to burn in the sun and be nibbled by insects and torn apart by coyotes. He knew that the Apaches did not take scalps but they did bury living enemies up to their necks in the ground and lather their faces with *tiswin*—corn liquor—in order to attract killer ants that ate out their eyeballs and invaded their noses and ears.

After school Roy asked Jimmy Boyle what he thought the Apaches would have done and Jimmy said, "Are you kiddin'? Those young bucks wouldn't leave a pretty girl to rot. Not once they seen her legs."

DARK AND BLACK AND STRANGE

As a boy, Roy often stayed up much of the night watching movies on TV. Most of them were old, black and white films from the 1930s and '40s. When he and his mother were living in hotels in Miami, Havana or New Orleans, she was usually out during the late night and early morning hours, leaving Roy by himself, which he did not mind; when they were in Chicago, staying at his grandmother's house, he had a little television in his room to watch the all-night movies on channel nine, a local station that owned an extensive archive of classic as well as obscure films.

The movies Roy preferred were mystery, crime and horror pictures such as *The End of Everything*, *Stairway to Doom*, *Three-and-a-Half Jealous Husbands*, *Fanged Sphinx of Fez*, and *Demented Darlings*. By far his favorite was *Snake Girl*, starring Arleena Mink, a purportedly Eurasian actress of uncertain provenance, who never made another movie. Unlike *Cult of the Cobra*, also one of Roy's favorites, which featured a woman who turned into a viper in order to commit murders, *Snake Girl* was about a child abandoned, supposedly by her parents, in a swamp for unexplained reasons.

When first we see Arleena Mink, an exotic-looking, stunningly beautiful teenage girl, unclothed but covered in strategic places by what appears to be a sheer coating of dark moss, her amazingly long, dark hair entwined around her neck, upper arms, waist and legs, she is not really walking but *gliding* in a dreary landscape both jungle and swamp. She deftly navigates her way through and beneath hanging moss and reptilian vines, sinuously evading gigantic Venus flytrap types of plants and overgrown vegetation. The only noises come from invisible birds that constantly squawk and screech. Her passage is interrupted briefly by an apparent flashback showing a car stopping on a road next to a swamp, the right front passenger door opening, and a person's hands and arms holding and then rolling a bundle—presumably containing the body of an infant—down an incline into the murk. The door closes and the car is driven on. We do not see the driver or passenger's faces.

Arleena Mink does not utter a sound other than an occasional hiss. Four men carrying rifles, machetes and nets appear, attired in khaki bush jackets and safari hats. They don't talk much as they plod past waving leaves and wade through brackish shallows. We assume they are hunting for the snake girl, whose existence, we learn from their minimal dialogue, may be only a rumor. Having seen Arleena Mink, however, we know her presence in the swampland is not a myth and she is apparently endeavoring to avoid capture.

Arleena slithers, slinks and crawls as her pursuers become increasingly frustrated due to biting insects, unidentified moving things rippling the waters, and debilitating heat. The action concludes when one after another of the men are eliminated: the first two sucked under and swallowed by quicksand, the third strangled by a serpent-vine, and the fourth dragged into dense foliage by the hairy arm of an otherwise unseen beast, the victim's cry muffled by one huge, sharp-clawed paw.

The snake girl may or may not have even been aware that she was being stalked by men; behaving cautiously is her natural condition. In the last shot of the movie she rises to her full height, stares directly into the camera, her slanted eyes burning and sparkling like black diamonds, and from between her puffy lips darts a shockingly long, whiplike tongue. The forked tip of Arleena Mink's quivering organ flaps and twists as she emits a sudden, deliciously hideous, spine-shriveling hiss.

Whenever Roy saw *Snake Girl* listed in a TV movie guide—without exception in the middle of the night—he watched it. Arleena Mink disappeared from public display after 1944, the year her one film was made. It wasn't until almost fifty years later that by chance Roy noticed an obituary in *Variety* that read: "Arleena Mink, actress, born Consuelina Norma Lagarto in Veracruz, Mexico, on January 1, 1930, died June 20 in Asunción, Paraguay. Her husband, Generalissimo Emilio Buenaventura-Schmid, whom she married when she was fifteen years old, preceded her in death, date unknown. Miss Mink's only film appearance was in *Snake Girl*, rumored to have been secretly directed in Brazil by Orson Welles, using the name Mauricio de Argentina. Writing in *Le Monde* (Paris), the eminent critic Edmund Wilson described *Snake Girl* as 'an erotic masterpiece, uniquely dark and black and strange. One can easily imagine being bitten by the vixenish, barely pubescent Arleena Mink and expiring without regret.'"

THE VAGARIES OF INCOMPLETENESS

After they moved from Florida to Chicago, Roy's mother hired a maid named Wilda Cherokee. Wilda, a sweet-tempered woman in her mid-twenties, had a son, Henry, who, like Roy, was seven years old. When Wilda could find nobody to take care of Henry, which was often, she brought him with her to Roy and his mother's house. After Roy came home from school he and Henry played together. Roy asked him if he ever got in trouble with his school for being absent so much and Henry said, "Not so much trouble as when I'm there."

"How come your last name is the name of an Indian tribe?" Roy asked.

"My mother's people are from North Carolina," Henry said. "They're part Indians."

Roy wished he had a great name like Cherokee and whenever he introduced Henry to someone he always said, "This is Henry Cherokee," not just Henry.

"He ain't an Indian," said Roy's friend Tommy Cunningham, "he's a Negro."

"He's both," Roy said. "His great-great grandmother was married to a Cherokee chief."

"What was the chief's name?" asked Tommy.

"Wind-Runs-Behind-Him," said Henry.

"You're makin' that up."

"No, I'm not. My grandmama Florence told me."

Roy, Tommy and Henry were standing in the alley behind Roy's house. Roy and Henry had been playing catch with a taped up hardball when Tommy came out of Jimmy Boyle's backyard, which he'd been cutting through.

"How come you're here?" Tommy asked.

"His mother works for us," said Roy.

"What's her name, Princess Summer-Fall-Winter-Spring?"

"Wilda," said Henry.

"Can you do a war dance? Say somethin' in Cherokee,"

A red Studebaker crept slowly up the alley and parked a couple of houses away behind a garage.

"That's Mr. Anderson," said Roy.

He waved at the tall, fair-haired man who got out of the car and the man waved back. Mr. Anderson walked over to the boys.

"Hello, Roy. And you're Paulie Cunningham's son, aren't you? How's your dad? He hasn't been around Beeb's Tavern lately."

"He's in jail," said Tommy. "But my ma says he's gettin' out soon."

"Tell him Sven Anderson says hello and that the first one's on me."

"Yes, sir."

"And who's this?" Mr. Anderson said, looking at Henry.

"This is my friend Henry Cherokee," said Roy.

"Do you live around here, Henry?"

"No."

"His mother works for my mother," Roy said.

Mr. Anderson fingered a cigarette from an open pack of Lucky Strikes in his shirt pocket, put it between his lips, then took out a green book of matches with the name Beeb's written on it in white letters, and lit the Lucky.

"I hired a colored fella to work at the bottling plant," he said. "Two years ago, I guess it was. He was a good worker. After about six months he didn't show up one Monday, didn't call in either. Turned out he'd been shot and killed in a bar Saturday night before."

"Henry's part Indian," said Roy.

"His grandfather was a chief," said Tommy Cunningham.

"My great-great grandfather," said Henry. "His name was Wind-Runs-Behind-Him."

"That's poetry, that is," Mr. Anderson said. "Our names aren't nearly as colorful, or descriptive. He must have been a fast runner."

"I don't know," said Henry.

"Nice meeting you, Henry. It's not every day I get to meet the great grandson of an Indian chief."

Mr. Anderson walked back toward his garage.

"What's poetry?" asked Tommy.

"Words that rhyme," said Roy.

"Wind-Runs-Behind-Him don't rhyme."

"What's your father in jail for?" Henry asked.

Tommy, who was almost nine and a head taller than Henry, bent over and put his nose on top of Henry's and said, "He's a horse thief."

Roy thought Tommy might try to beat Henry up so he got ready to hit Tommy in his head with the hardball, but Tommy backed off and began running down the alley.

"Does his father really steal horses?" asked Henry.

The sky had clouded over in a hurry.

"Come on," said Roy, "let's play catch before it rains."

KING AND COUNTRY

In January of that year a monumental blizzard hit Chicago, forcing the city to shut down for four days. Virtually all businesses closed except for a few neighborhood bars and liquor stores. Only police, firefighters and emergency services remained available. Residents were advised not to try to drive; the only way around was on foot.

Roy was thirteen and by the night of the second day cabin fever compelled him to venture out to visit his friend Jimmy Boyle, who lived a couple of blocks away. Wading down the middle of Ojibway Boulevard through the hip-and even chest-high drifts, Roy encountered a man coming out of Beebs and Glen's Tavern carrying two fifths of Murphy's Irish whiskey, one under each arm.

"I'm goin' to Peggy Dean's house and I'm not comin' out for a week!" he shouted.

Just before Roy reached Jimmy's block another man came toward him, also struggling to make a path for himself. He was wearing a purple turban and wrapped around his body were layers of different colored robes, rags and rugs. The man's barely visible face was brown and bearded. He was pulling a two-wheeled cart laden with what Roy assumed were his belongings, piled high and covered with more rugs and pieces of material. As Roy and the man approached one another, Roy could see that beneath his robes, which reached to his ankles, the man was barefoot.

"Ah, I saw you from afar!" the man said to Roy, and stopped in front of him.

The man's eyes blazed like blue moons in the darkness.

"You look like a king," Roy said.

"I was a king in my own country," replied the man.

"Aren't you afraid your feet will get frostbite?"

"I come from a strong and powerful people who walk in the footsteps of Arphax, he who lived more than four-hundred years and paved a fiery path. My feet are like unto fine brass, as if they burn in a furnace. My servant Isaiah walked naked and barefoot for three years through a hostile and terrible land. Though I hath cometh out of prison to reign again am I also he who becometh poor."

The man began to move forward, dragging his cart.

"What's your name?" Roy called after him.

"To know me," said the man, "you must first solve the mystery of the seven stars."

When Roy got to Jimmy Boyle's house he told him about the biblical character who said he'd been a king in his own country.

"His name is Morris Jones," said Jimmy. "He used to be a fry cook at the Busy Bee on Milwaukee Avenue. He went batshit about a year ago and started tellin' everyone he was the son of God. He lives under the el over there. My father gives him a buck or two when he sees him."

"Is he dangerous?"

"He carries a carving knife under his robes. He took it from the diner. Elmer Schuh, who owns the Busy Bee, let him keep it to protect himself."

Roy did not see Morris Jones again until the following August. It was a boiling hot day and Morris was sitting in the back seat of a police car parked in front of the el station with his hands cuffed, wearing his purple turban. Roy asked a cop standing next to the car why Morris had been arrested.

"He carved up a dog and was tryin' to sell the parts to passengers gettin' on and off the trains."

"Is that against the law?"

"It is when you're not wearin' nothing but a turban."

"He was a king in his own country," Roy said.

"He should have stayed there," said the cop.

The next day Roy told Jimmy Boyle about his having seen Morris being arrested, and what for.

"He was naked?"

"Except for his turban."

"I don't think Morris would ever hurt anyone on purpose," said Jimmy. "He always gave me extra bacon whenever I went into the Busy Bee with my dad."

HOUSE OF BAMBOO

Roy was sitting at the kitchen table eating a ham and cheese sandwich when his mother appeared from the front of the house pushing Marty Bell toward the back door.

"I hope you don't mind going out this way, Marty," she said. "I thought it would be easier since you're parked in the alley."

Marty Bell was one of Roy's mother's boyfriends. He wanted to marry her but despite the fact that he made "a good living," as she said, Roy's mother would not marry him.

"Too bad he's so short," she had told Roy. "He only comes up to my shoulders. How could I be seen with him?"

Roy's mother allowed Marty Bell to kiss her on the cheek before he went out the back door. Just as she closed it behind him, the front doorbell rang. She hurried through the house to answer it and returned less than a minute later to the kitchen accompanied by Bill Crown, another boyfriend of hers. Bill Crown was considerably taller than Marty Bell. His right arm was wrapped around Roy's mother's shoulders, and she was smiling.

"Look, Roy, Bill brought you a present."

"Here," said Bill Crown, "you can practice with this."

With his left hand Bill handed Roy a small polo mallet. He knew that Crown played polo on the weekends, but Roy knew practically nothing about the sport, other than it was played on horseback and the participants rode around trying to hit a small, hard wooden ball into a goal. None of his friends knew anything about polo, either.

"I'd like you and your mother to come out to Oak Brook on Saturday to watch me play. It'll be a good match."

Bill took a scuffed white ball out of a pocket of his brown leather coat and set it on the table.

"This is from last week's match," he said. "You can knock it around the yard."

Roy put down his sandwich and held the mallet in both of his hands.

"Put your hand through the strap when you grip the handle. That way you won't drop the mallet. It's made of bamboo. It'll bend but won't break."

"Thanks," Roy said. "I have a baseball game on Saturday."

"We play on Sundays, too, sometimes. I'll let you know. You'll come this Saturday, Kitty, won't you?"

"I'll be happy to," said Roy's mother.

She and Bill Crown left the kitchen. Roy placed the mallet on the floor and finished eating his sandwich.

The next day, Roy was batting the wooden ball around in front of his house when his friend Johnny Murphy came by.

"What kind of a club is that?" asked Johnny.

"A polo mallet. Bill Crown, a friend of my mother's, gave it to me. You ride horses and sock this ball with it."

Roy handed Johnny the mallet.

"The shaft is made from bamboo and the head is hard wood, like the ball."

"Sounds like hockey."

"Yeah, only on horseback."

"I think just rich guys play polo," Johnny said. "Maybe he'll give you a horse."

"Uh huh. We can keep it in our apartment."

"Is your mother gonna marry him?"

"I don't know."

"How many times has she been married?"

"Twice."

"My mother says it's rough on kids who come from broken homes. Do you want this guy to be your father?"

"I have a father. I've only seen Bill Crown a couple of times. He's okay."

Johnny hit the ball and it rolled into the street.

"What does your mother like about him?"

"He's tall," Roy said, and went to get the ball.

THE UNEXPECTED

"You think Miss Peaches is terrific, you shoulda seen Little Egypt that time Gus Argo and I were in East Saint Louis at Miss Vivian's Evening in Havana."

"The original Little Egypt was a Syrian dame made her bones at the Columbian Exposition in 1890-somethin'. Married a Greek guy owned a restaurant. Other girls stole the name and her act, only they done it dirtier."

Roy was in Meschina's Delicatessen sitting in a booth with Jewish Joe, who wasn't Jewish, and Al Martin, who was. Roy ran errands for the men when he needed extra money. He was fourteen years old, Joe and Al were both in their forties. They'd done time for making book and extortion, but they never involved Roy or any of the other kids who worked for them in anything the kids knew was illegal. Mostly the men used the boys to deliver messages to people when they didn't want to use a telephone. The messages were in code. Joe or Al would tell a kid to go over to the Time Out, a bar on South Mohawk, and tell Big Lloyd, the bartender, "Ali Baba had twenty-five thieves, not forty." The kid would keep a few newspapers under one arm to make out like he was a newsboy in case any no good law was around, and Big Lloyd would say, "No minors or peddlers allowed, kid. Take the air."

For this or similar endeavors, Roy would get five bucks. He got a kick out of the gangster talk but he didn't consider Jewish Joe or

Al Martin real mobsters. They were small-timers hustling a living. Chicago was full of guys like them. Roy figured it was the same in any big city and so long as he didn't have knowledge of any of the particulars he wouldn't get in trouble.

One Friday night Al Martin handed Roy a menu from Meschina's and told him to take it to 1432 Water Street. A woman would answer the door, a blonde in her late twenties, and Roy should give her the menu. On the way over to Water Street, which was a good sixteen blocks from Meschina's, Roy examined the menu and saw at the bottom of the second page a telephone number written in pencil. Al said if anybody other than the blonde opened the door Roy should say he'd made a mistake and bring the menu back to Meschina's.

"What if somebody chases me?" Roy asked.

"Run," said Al. "Don't drop the menu."

Roy lived with his mother and younger sister. His father was dead. Roy's mother worked as a receptionist at a hospital and Roy worked three nights a week delivering Chinese food on a bicycle. He gave half of the money he made from the Chinese restaurant to his mother. She didn't know he ran errands for Joe and Al.

He knocked on the door at 1432 Water but nobody answered right away. It was a cool, windy night, and Roy had not minded the long walk. Jewish Joe and Al Martin and every other denizen of Meschina's smoked cigarettes and cigars even while they ate, so Roy was glad to be out in the fresh air. He did not smoke because when he began boxing at the YMCA two years before his trainer, Pat Touhy, told him, as he told all the boys, not to smoke, drink alcohol or lift weights.

"When you roll out of the sack in the morning," Pat Touhy instructed, "get down on the floor and do a hundred sit-ups and as many fingertip push-ups as you can, then go take a piss and brush your teeth. Don't touch a weight or your muscles will tighten up. I want you long and loose and fast. Weight work cuts quickness. And you run—run to school, to the gym, to work. Walkin's a waste of motion."

Roy knocked again and this time a woman opened the door but she was a brunette and she looked a lot older than twenty-something. Roy heard a man's voice from inside ask, "Who's there, Phyllis?"

"I made a mistake, lady," said Roy. "I got the wrong house."

He walked away but before he'd gone fifteen steps someone came up behind him and said, "Did Al send you?"

Roy turned around and saw a blonde woman with a bad complexion who looked even older than the brunette who had opened the door. The blonde's face was vaguely familiar.

"What are you holding?" she asked.

Roy wasn't sure what to do. He looked back at the house; the front door was open and the dark-haired woman was standing on the sidewalk watching him and the other woman.

"Is that for me?" said the blonde, pointing at the menu in Roy's left hand.

"Al Martin sent you, didn't he?"

"How old are you?" asked Roy.

The woman hesitated a moment before saying, "What do you care?"

A man came out of the house, brushed past the brunette and walked toward Roy and the blonde. Roy did not recognize him. The man was mostly bald and was wearing an unbuttoned white shirt with the sleeves rolled up to his elbows. He was holding a gun in his right hand against his right leg. Roy turned and ran. After he'd gone four blocks he stopped and looked back. Nobody was chasing him.

Jewish Joe and Al Martin were still at their table in Meschina's when Roy came in. He put the menu down in front of Al.

"Nobody home?" Al said.

"A brunette answered the door, then a bleached blonde about forty years old came out and wanted what I had that you'd given me."

"Yeah, then what?"

"A bald guy came out of the house carrying a gun, so I took off."

"A bald guy," said Joe. "Kind of heavy?"

"I guess so. Maybe. I saw the piece, I ran."

"Sorry about that," said Al.

He reached a hand inside his suit jacket, took out a billfold, opened it, removed two fives and handed them to Roy.

"Why the extra fin?" Roy asked.

"The unexpected."

"I got scared when I saw the guy had a gun."

"Sure you did," said Jewish Joe.

"Okay, kid, go home," said Al Martin. "See you next Friday."

Roy looked in both directions on the street in front of Meschina's. The temperature had dropped and sweat dried cold under his shirt. The blonde used to do the weather report on channel two. She looked better on TV.

THE WAY OF ALL FLESH

"You boys know about Oriental girls? Their slits go sideways, so you have to prop 'em up perpendicular to yourself goin' in or you'll have a bent pecker comin' out."

Roy and Eddie Hay were standing under the awning outside Myron and Jerry's Steakhouse on South Mohawk getting the goods from Sonny Lightfoot. Sonny worked for Jib Bufera, who ate lunch every afternoon except Sunday at three o'clock at Myron and Jerry's. Sonny's real last name was Veronesi, but he earned his nickname when he weighed forty pounds less and burglarized houses while the residents were sleeping. He became famous for his ability to tread so softly that nobody woke up while he pilfered jewelry and other valuables. These days he drove for Jib Bufera.

"Jib's got me on call twenty out of twenty-four, so I snooze in the Lincoln while he's havin' meetings."

"You like workin' for Jib?" asked Eddie Hay, who the other boys called Hey Eddie, which he hated.

"Can't complain. Less stressful than breakin' and enterin'. Jib's generous. He and his goombahs speak Sicilian most of the time, which is okay by me because then I don't know nothin' when the wrong guys ask me what I know."

A steady, warm rain had put an early end to the boys' ballgame but Roy did not mind since he was fighting a summer cold.

"Hey Eddie," he said, "I'm goin' home. Take it easy, Sonny. And thanks for the anatomy lesson."

"Any time, kid. Shake that cold."

Roy was twelve years old and didn't know much about girls. He had his doubts, though, about Sonny Lightfoot being a source of reliable information.

When he got home, Roy's grandfather was asleep in an armchair with a book on his lap. Roy looked at the title: *Germany Will Try It Again.* He went into his room and turned on the little red and white portable TV he kept on a table next to his bed, then took off his shoes and lay down. There was an old movie on about a terminally ill man, a philosophy professor, who decides to do the world a favor and murder a truly evil person before he himself dies. The professor shoots and kills a spider woman who is having an affair with the husband of a colleague of his. The spider woman is a crook who has seduced the husband, an artist, and blackmailed him into creating paintings in the styles of old masters and selling them as lost or stolen masterpieces to private collectors. The professor confesses his crime to the police, goes to trial and is sentenced to die in the electric chair. Before he is executed, however, the professor is horrified to learn that another man, having read in a newspaper about the professor's reason for committing the murder, has subscribed to the professor's philosophy and mistakenly killed an innocent person.

The spider woman, when confronted by the professor, was unmoved by his plea that she relinquish her hold on the husband. Her smug, nonchalant attitude infuriated him but intrigued Roy. If a diabolical but goodlooking dame like this got her hooks into a man, he realized, she could compel him to do almost anything.

Roy's grandfather appeared in the doorway.

"Hello, Roy. I didn't hear you come in."

"Hi, Pops. You were sleeping. I didn't want to disturb you."

"Are you hungry?"

"No, I'm okay. Pops, do you think there are people who are really evil? Or are they just mentally ill?"

"I'm sorry to say, Roy, I believe in the existence of evil. Hitler, for example, was an evil man who had the ability to inspire and manipulate people into committing the most gruesome acts of villainy."

"I saw the book you're reading about Germany. Hitler was a German, wasn't he?"

"No, he was Austrian, but he became chancellor of Germany."

"There had to be a lot of evil people in Germany to do what they did."

"That's what the book is about. The author theorizes that their society is genetically predisposed to waging war, that they possess an imperative biological desire to control others and force them to submit to their will."

"A woman can do that to a man."

"Yes, and a man can do it to a woman."

"How much does sex have to do with it?"

"Sometimes everything, sometimes nothing. Do you have any more questions before I make myself a sandwich?"

"Just one, but it can wait."

"What's it about?"

"Oriental girls."

SOME PRODUCTS OF THE IMAGINATION

Roy did not realize he was lost until a woman hanging wash on a line in her backyard asked him what he was doing there. Roy was walking home alone from kindergarten. It had been his second day at school and he had decided to take a shortcut through the alley between Washtenaw and Minnetonka streets and then cut through a yard to get to Minnetonka.

"Where are you going, little boy?" the woman asked him.

Sheets and towels on the line were fluttering in the wind and the sun was half-blinding him.

"Home."

"What street do you live on?"

"I'm not trying to steal anything, lady. I was just cutting through."

"You don't look like a thief. What's your name?"

"Roy. I live on Rockwell, with my mother."

One of the sheets kept flapping up in Roy's face so he ducked under it and stood directly in front of the woman, who seemed very big. She was wearing a gray and white checked housecoat, and her long black hair was being blown back and forth across her face.

"Well, Roy, Rockwell is one block over. Is your house closer to Ojibway or to Minnetonka?"

"Ojibway."

"Then you'll turn left on Rockwell."

"Can I walk through your yard or should I go back to the alley?"

"Of course you can walk through the yard. How old are you?"

"Five."

"You're very young to be walking to or from school by yourself. It's more than half a mile from your house."

"I can do it. I just got confused trying to take a shortcut."

"My name is Mrs. Miller, Roy. You can cut through my yard whenever you want to."

"Thanks. Do you have a dog?"

"No, no dog."

When Roy got home nobody was there. Both his mother and grandmother, who was visiting from Miami, were out. His mother had left a note for him on the kitchen table.

> *Roy, I hope you had a good day at school. Nanny and I have gone downtown to buy her a coat. She is not used to the cold weather in Chicago. There is roast beef left over from last night's dinner in the refrigerator. Make yourself a sandwich if you are hungry. The bread is in the bread box. Drink a glass of milk. Nanny and I will be home soon.*
>
> *Mom*

Roy wasn't hungry, so he went into his room and lay down on the bed. The next thing he knew his mother was sitting on the bed talking to him.

"Hi, sweetheart. Did you eat something?"

"No, I guess I was too tired. I dreamed I was lost in a desert and the wind was blowing sand around so I couldn't see very well and then a beautiful lady appeared out of the sand and held my hand and led me out of the desert."

"Did you recognize this beautiful lady, Roy? Was it me?"

"No, she had black hair."

"Did she tell you her name?"

"Yes, it was Mrs. Miller."

Both Roy's mother and grandmother, who had come into the room, laughed.

"Maybe Mrs. Miller was a mirage," said his mother.

"What's a mirage?"

"Something you think you see but it's not really there. It's a product of the imagination."

"How do you like my new coat, Roy?" his grandmother asked. She was wearing a bright pink coat.

"Anyone can see me in this," she said, "especially drivers when I'm crossing a busy street."

"Tell me if you want to eat something," said his mother.

She smoothed his hair back off his forehead, then she stood up and both women left Roy's room.

On his way home from school the next afternoon, Roy opened the back gate to Mrs. Miller's yard, closed it behind him, and was about to walk through when a man came out of the back door of the house and said, "Where do you think you're going?"

The man was very big, bigger than Mrs. Miller, and he had a mean look on his face. He walked toward Roy.

"Mrs. Miller said I could cut through her yard on my way home from school."

"If I see you in this yard again, I'll let my dog out."

The man's head was completely bald and red. His face and eyes were red, too. Roy backed away, opened the gate and stepped into the alley.

"What happened to Mrs. Miller?" he asked.

"Something will happen to you and any of your friends if I catch you in here."

"She said she didn't have a dog."

The man pulled on the gate and closed it with a loud clang, then he turned around and stomped back to the house.

Each day for the rest of that week Roy stopped in the alley and looked into the yard but Mrs. Miller was never there. After that, he walked home a different way.

About a month later, Roy was with his mother on Ojibway Boulevard when he saw Mrs. Miller walking toward them. He was about to say hello but Mrs. Miller passed by without looking at him. Roy stopped and looked back at her. She was holding a big brown dog on a leash.

Roy remained curious about Mrs. Miller and the man who had kicked him out of the yard. Why did she tell him she didn't have a dog? Roy decided to go back one more time to ask her. He stood in the alley behind the Miller house and waited for twenty minutes before the back door opened and the brown dog bounded down the steps followed by Mrs. Miller.

Roy went up to the fence and said, "Mrs. Miller? Can I talk to you?"

She came over to the fence, as did the dog.

"Hello, Roy. I haven't seen you for a long time."

"I tried to cut through your yard one day and a man came out and told me I couldn't. He said if I tried to again he would let his dog out to attack me. I told him you said I could and that you said you didn't have a dog. After that, I saw you on Ojibway Boulevard walking with this dog."

Mrs. Miller smiled and said, "I'm sorry for the confusion, Roy. The man is my brother, Eugene. He was staying here for a few days. He lives in St. Louis. This is his dog, Grisby. Eugene went back to St. Louis and left Grisby with me until he finds a new place to live. I'm afraid Grisby isn't properly socialized, so it's probably a good idea while I have him here that you don't cut through the yard. He might bite you."

"Okay, I won't."

"I'm sorry, Roy. I don't think he'll be here too much longer, though I don't mind having his company."

Grisby propped his large front paws on top of the fence and barked at Roy. He had a long, green tongue and sharp teeth.

"Your brother is scary," Roy said.

"He's had a difficult life, Roy. I'm trying to help him out."

"Was he ever in prison?"

Mrs. Miller stared at Roy for a few moments before answering.

"Yes, as a matter of fact, he was. How could you know? Did Eugene tell you?"

"Was it for murder?"

"I think you'd better go home now, Roy."

Grisby got down from the fence and followed her. Roy noticed that part of the dog's tail was missing; it looked as if half of it had been chopped off.

Just as he arrived at his house, Roy's mother ran out and shouted something Roy could not hear clearly at his grandmother, who was standing in the doorway. He watched his mother get into her car without saying anything to him and drive away.

"What happened, Nanny?" he asked. "Where's my mother going?"

"I couldn't stop her, Roy. Like most really beautiful women, she's often overwhelmed by her insecurities."

"I don't know what that means."

"It doesn't matter. Come into the house."

"Is she in trouble?"

"I hope not."

"Mrs. Miller is really beautiful and I think she's in trouble."

"Who's Mrs. Miller?"

"I told you and Mom about her. Her brother Eugene is a murderer. He escaped from prison and killed Mrs. Miller's husband."

THE COMEDIAN

On the hottest day of the summer Roy and his friend Elmo Rubinsky played Fast Ball at the schoolyard. It was a two man game, one pitching, one batting, exchanging places after three outs in an inning. The pitcher threw to a box marked in chalk on a brick wall; this was the strike zone. Lines were drawn in the gravel on the ground behind the pitcher; a ball hit past him on the fly was a single, past the first line was a double, against the fence was a triple, over the fence a home run. Foul lines were drawn on both sides of the field. The pitcher called balls and strikes; often, if the batter protested a call, it didn't count and the pitcher had to throw it again.

After their game was over, the boys were exhausted and dehydrated, so they staggered over to the Standard gas station two blocks away to buy bottles of cold Nehi soda pop for a nickel apiece from a machine inside the station waiting room. Elmo had won the game that day largely due to his use of what he called his "back up" pitch, which looked to the batter like a fast ball but appeared to slow down—or back up—after the batter had already begun his swing, causing him to pop up the ball or miss it entirely.

Elmo drank half a dozen grape sodas and Roy half a dozen orange. The sports section of that morning's *Tribune* was on a table in the waiting room where Roy and Elmo sat on wooden folding chairs draining Nehis from the bottles. Roy examined the box scores from the previous day's major league baseball games and saw that a rookie on the San Francisco Giants named Willie McCovey had made his debut by going four for four, hitting two triples and two singles. This was the first game of what turned out to be McCovey's hall of fame career.

Across the street from the gas station was a synagogue and when the boys looked out the window of the waiting room they saw that a crowd was gathering on the sidewalk in front of the steps leading to the entrance. After they had finished the last of their bottles of pop, Roy and Elmo left the station and went across the street to find out what was going on.

"We're waitin' for George Burns to arrive," said a kid. "The rabbi here died and his funeral is today. George Burns was his brother and he's supposed to be comin' in from New York or Hollywood for the burial."

George Burns was a famous comedian. He and his wife, Gracie Allen, had acted in many movies and currently had a popular television show. The crowd had gathered not necessarily out of respect for the deceased rabbi but to see if it was true that George Burns was his brother and that he would show up for the funeral. Most of the people waiting around were not Jewish and had never been inside the synagogue nor did they even know the name of George Burns's brother. Elmo asked a man what the rabbi's name was and he said, "Birnbaum. George's real name is Nathan Birnbaum. He changed it to George Burns because he was in show business, because of anti-Semitism. He didn't want people to know he was a Jew."

The crowd surged to the curb as a long, black limousine pulled over and stopped. The driver got out, came around the car and opened the curbside rear passenger door. George Burns got out, holding a big cigar in his right hand. He was a very small man;

he smiled and waved. He wore glasses and a bad toupée. People shouted his name over and over and shouted, "Where's Gracie?" Everyone was genuinely excited to see that it really was the famous comedian.

George Burns and his brother had grown up in New York City. They were from a poor family that lived on the Lower East Side. Nathan had become an entertainer when he was very young, beginning his career in vaudeville, eventually changing his name and moving to Hollywood. Some people in the crowd tried to get his autograph but his chauffeur pushed through the throng clearing a path ahead of the comedian and the two of them went up the steps of the synagogue and disappeared inside. Two police cars drove up and parked behind the limousine. Two uniformed cops got out of each car and waded into the crowd, telling people to move away from the synagogue entrance.

Nobody left; they were determined to wait until George Burns came out so they could see him smile and wave his cigar at them again. A black hearse pulled up and stopped in the middle of the street. Roy and Elmo crossed the street to get away from the people pushing and shoving one another in order to be in better positions to watch the mourners leave for the cemetery. More cars came and parked in a line behind the hearse.

Two mechanics from the gas station came out from the garage and stood on the sidewalk with Roy and Elmo. The name patches on their coveralls were Rip and Don.

"I didn't know George Burns was a Jew," said Rip.

"I like his wife on the show," said Don. "She's always getting' things mixed up and he stands around holdin' a big cigar and explains what she said."

"I know a guy named Bill Burns," Rip said. "He's a Lutheran."

Roy and Elmo did not wait to see George Burns come back

164

out. They were walking to Elmo's house when he said, "What if George Burns changed his name back to Birnbaum now? He's sixty years old or older and famous, not just starting out, so he shouldn't be worried about anti-Semites preventing him from getting work. Everyone knows who George Burns is, right? Everyone in the entertainment business knows he's a Jew. So do his fans."

"Rip, the grease monkey at the Standard station, didn't know."

"It would be an important statement against anti-Semitism, I think," said Elmo.

"You should write him a letter," Roy said, "and tell him that."

When the boys got to the house Elmo's father was in the gangway digging up dirt around his tomato plants. Elmo told him his idea and that Roy had suggested he write to George Burns. Big Sol Rubinsky owned a salvage business on the south side of Chicago and had fought in the Pacific with the Marines during World War II.

"Them guys don't think like that," he said. "You'd just be wastin' a stamp."

The next day Roy read in the *Sun-Times* that George Burns had been in town for his brother's funeral. The article said that due to personal differences the brothers had not talked to or seen each other in many years. When asked the reasons for their estrangement, George Burns was quoted as saying the only difference between them was that his brother did not smoke cigars.

LAMENT FOR A DAUGHTER OF EGYPT

When he was a small boy, Roy's mother liked to throw parties. She was a good dancer, especially of the Latin variety such as the samba, mambo and cha-cha-cha. After her divorce from Roy's father, when Roy was five years old, his mother invited several couples to their apartment on Saturday nights every other week or so. Her own companions during the three years between the divorce and her second marriage were a succession of over-smiling, iron-hand-shaking, smooth-dancing guys who were always surprised that she had a child. It was obvious to Roy that she had not mentioned his existence to any of them prior to the evenings of her parties.

On one of these occasions, while her guests were shuffling tip-sily to Art Blakey's "Jodie's Cha-cha," Roy's mother and her date, a broad-shouldered, slick-haired man with a dark brown paint-smear mustache named Bob Arno, got into a tiff over his having danced once too often with someone's wife. Roy usually hung out on the periphery observing the action. His mother's wrangling with Arno began in the kitchen, where he was in the process of mixing himself a drink, then continued into the diningroom before ending abruptly in the front hall, where he hammered the remainder of his cocktail, handed the empty glass to her and left the apartment.

Three women immediately surrounded Roy's mother, each of them chattering like monkeys about the incident, indicting the wife as the instigator. A tall, blonde woman appeared in the hallway, a mink stole draped around her otherwise bare shoulders, said good night to the other women and made a swift exit. A few seconds later, a husky man in a baggy gray suit approached them.

"Have you seen Helen?" he asked.

His face was green and his eyes were bloodshot.

"I believe she just went out to get a pack of cigarettes," said Kay O'Connor, a skinny redhead about whom Roy had once heard his mother say never left her house without make-up on and a gun in her purse.

"Helen doesn't smoke," said the man.

"Come on, Marty," Roy's mother said to him, "let's dance."

She handed Bob Arno's empty glass to Roy, took one of the man's hands and led him into the livingroom.

"Didn't you used to date Bob Arno?" one of the women asked Kay O'Connor.

"He's afraid of me," Kay said.

"You mean he's afraid of Harvey," said the third woman.

"What's the diff?" said Kay.

The three women walked into the livingroom.

Roy watched his mother doing the cha-cha with the husky man. His face had turned from green to bright red and Roy's mother was laughing, showing all of her teeth.

After the cha-cha number ended, someone put on another record. A woman's voice, high-pitched with a tremble in it, delivered the song's lyrics slowly and directly, but somehow a half-step behind the band without dragging the beat. Everyone stopped talking and laughing and listened.

"I still remember/the first time you said/If I can't be free/I'd rather be dead/Now that you're gone/and nothing has changed/the answer to my question/can be arranged."

Somebody took off the record and put on a mambo and people started talking and laughing again. Roy went to the kitchen, put the glass in the sink, then went to his room and closed the door.

The next morning, he asked his mother if she thought it had been a good party.

"Not all bad," she said, "but not all good, either."

"Are you going to see Mr. Arno again?"

His mother reached far back into a cabinet, found a clean cup, and poured coffee for herself. The kitchen was a mess.

"He's not in our plans any more, I don't think," she said. "You don't like him, anyway, do you, Roy?"

THE OLD WEST

Like most young boys in the 1950s, Roy often wondered what it would have been like to have lived in the Old West. Movies and television shows mostly glorified those days, despite frontier lawlessness and having to fight hostile Indians. The reality that not many people lived into let alone past their thirties did not enter into Roy's thinking; to a seven or eight year old, thirty or more years might as well be two hundred. Neither did the idea of men killing one another without remorse deter Roy and his playmates in the least. Growing up in Chicago, they were used to hearing and reading about gangsters strangling and shooting their adversaries; also, most of the boys were sons of men who had fought in World War II, some of whom had been wounded or had brothers who died in battle. Violent death was a not unfamiliar circumstance, nor was it devoid of meaning; but this did not preclude their pantomiming violence in their fantasy scenarios.

Rube Danko, a ten year old cousin of Roy's friend Billy Katz, had, thanks to Billy, the reputation of being an exceptionally fast draw. Danko lived in a rough neighborhood, and Billy bragged about how tough his cousin was. When Billy brought him around one day, Roy was surprised that even though Rube was a couple of years older, he was short and pudgy. Danko didn't look tough and had a seemingly permanent grin on his puffy-cheeked face. He did not say much, and agreed to participate in whatever games his cousin and the other boys were playing. Danko wore a shiny silver and black gunbelt and badly scuffed brown and white cowboy boots, a black cowboy hat, blue jeans and a green T-shirt with the words Logan Square Boys Club written on it in white lettering.

Jimmy Boyle, Tommy Cunningham and Roy were the good guys; Katz, Danko and Murphy were the bad guys. Following a big shootout, only two boys were left standing: Roy and Rube Danko. The final showdown was between them, a quick-draw gunfight. Whoever pulled their gun and fired first won; the losers would then have to buy cokes for everyone.

Roy and Danko faced off ten feet apart. Katz's cousin was grinning, fingering the butt of his gun. Roy drew, pointed his revolver at Rube and shouted, "Bang!" Danko did not draw, just stood there smiling. Finally, he pulled his pistol and fired it twice into the air.

"Don't worry," he said, "they're blanks, and I'll buy the Cokes."

Later that day, after Rube had left, Jimmy Boyle said to Billy Katz, "Your cousin is weird. What if those bullets weren't really blanks?"

"His father works for the government," said Billy. "The FBI, maybe. I'm not sure. The gun must belong to him."

"Did you know it was real?" Roy asked.

Katz shook his head.

"The kid's crazy," said Tommy. "Why's he always smiling?"

Johnny Murphy pushed Billy in his chest and said, "Don't bring him around to play with us any more."

A couple of years later, Billy told Roy that his cousin Rube had gotten killed playing Russian Roulette.

"He was probably smiling when he pulled the trigger," Roy said.

INCURABLE

"Your father was a very generous man. He'd give you the shirt off his back, if he liked you. But in business he was tough, even ruthless; nobody got the better of him. Your mother shouldn't have divorced him; but then she shouldn't have married him, either."

Roy and his Uncle Buck, his mother's brother, were riding in Buck's Cadillac convertible on Dale Mabry Boulevard in Tampa, Florida, having just inspected a prospective site for a housing project Buck's company, Gulf Construction, was considering for development. Roy was thirteen years old; his father had been dead for almost two years. Since his parents had divorced when Roy was five, he had not known his father as well as he would have liked. During most of his childhood, Buck had been the primary paternal figure and influence in Roy's life.

"Were you and my dad friends?"

"We were friendly. He was only one year older but he had been in business since he was very young, so he was more experienced. I was just getting started as a civil engineer when your mother married him; and then for the first two years they were together I was up in the Yukon building the railroad. He knew most of the important people in Chicago, he made a good living. Your father made sure your mother had whatever she wanted and she enjoyed the nightlife. He was a twenty-four hour kind of guy."

"He was much older than my mother."

"Fifteen years older. He was good to her, and he really loved you."

"Why didn't Nanny like him?"

"Your grandmother didn't dislike him, Roy. She was just protective of your mother. She was afraid of some of the people your dad did business with."

"I met a lot of those guys. They were nice to me."

"Why shouldn't they have been? You were a little boy and nobody wanted to get on the wrong side of your father."

"Nanny said they were dangerous."

"Even after your parents were divorced, if my mother had a problem she called your dad."

"Did he always fix it?"

"He loved your mother, so I'm sure he did what he could."

"I remember once when a guy my mother didn't want to see any more kept calling her and coming around, and Nanny said to her, 'If you don't call Rudy to take care of him, I will.'"

"There's a good Cuban place up here, La Teresita. Feel like eating?"

"Sure."

Buck pulled the Caddy into the parking lot of the restaurant. The sun was going down and when they got out of the car a strong breeze was blowing in off the Gulf.

"Just a minute, Roy. I'm going to put up the top in case it rains."

"I'll do it, Unk."

Roy slid into the driver's seat, turned the key in the ignition and pushed the button that controlled the top. Once it was up, he fastened both the driver's and passenger's sides, turned the key off, removed it, got out and handed the key to his uncle. The wind felt good and Roy stood still for a moment watching the sky turn different shades of red. This was one of the best things about Florida, he thought, the sunsets.

His mother had had three husbands since she divorced his father. Roy felt better when he was with his uncle. They went fishing together and Roy worked on construction jobs for him. Buck taught him about navigation, mineralogy, the correct way to build a staircase and the architecture of bridges. He treated Roy differently than other men, not exactly as an equal, but Roy felt that he could trust him, that he could talk to his uncle about almost anything.

"I don't think I'll ever get married," Roy said.

Buck's first wife had divorced him and Roy knew that his uncle's second marriage was on the rocks.

" 'Weak you will find it in one only part, now pierced by love's incurable dart.'"

"What's that?"

"Lines from a sonnet by John Milton. I had to memorize it when I was in high school. Do you remember Rameses Thompson, who used to work for me?"

"The black guy who had a holster for his handgun on the inside of the driver's side door of his pickup truck. Is he still around?"

"No. He killed his common-law wife, Rosita, and her girlfriend."

"His wife had a girlfriend?"

"They were stepsisters, from Panama City. Thompson got caught in Mobile, Alabama, and a cop shot him in his spine. I hear he's alive but can't use his arms or legs."

"He was very strong. He could lift two chairs at the same time holding each one by only one leg."

"Rosita was ugly and lazy, but Thompson was crazy about her."

Another thing Roy liked about the west coast of Florida was that rain was never far away. It started a few minutes after he and his uncle were inside La Teresita.

SHRIMPERS

Roy and his friend Willy Duda were looking for a summer job. They were both fourteen years old and temporary work that paid decently in Tampa, Florida, in 1961, was hard to find. Tampa was a small southern city then, a fishing and cigar town with a large ethnic Cuban population. Roy's uncle Buck, with whom Roy lived during the summer months, was in the construction business; he would have employed both his nephew and Willy Duda, as he had in better times, but the building trade was slow at the moment so the boys had to look elsewhere to make money. Buck, who had been a lieutenant commander in the navy during the second world war, suggested they sign up to work on a shrimp boat.

"These little boats have small crews," Buck told them, "usually only the captain and two or three helpers. The boats go out for ten days, two weeks, maybe three at most, then bring in their catch, sell it, take a few days off, and go back out again. Come on, I'll take you down to the docks and we'll see if someone needs hands."

Roy and Willy didn't know anything about shrimping but Roy's uncle said the work was pretty simple. It was a cloudless, sunny day, as usual, and Buck talked while he drove.

"You toss out the nets into the shrimp beds, haul 'em in and load 'em in a cooler. It's repetitious, hard work, and there's nothing to do but work on a shrimp boat in the middle of the Gulf of Mexico. You sleep on deck."

"It's hot as Hades out there," said Willy. "We'll fry like catfish being on the water twenty-four hours a day."

"You boys can hold up for a fortnight," Buck said. "It'll be a good experience."

The shrimp boats docked under the Simon Bolívar Bridge. Roy's uncle drove his 1957 Cadillac Eldorado convertible right onto the wharf, parked, and he and the two boys got out. Most of the boats were empty or their captains were asleep under a canopy. Buck, Willy and Roy walked along the wooden planks until they came upon a man in a boat mending nets. The boat's name, painted on the stern in faded black letters, was *Lazarus*.

"Ahoy there, captain," Roy's uncle called out to him. "I've got a couple of strong young men here looking for work. Are you hiring?"

The man had a lobster-red face with a six day beard and a dead cigar sticking out of the right side of his mouth. Roy thought he looked to be about forty years old, maybe older. The man's left eye was closed and did not open during the time he spoke to them. He was wearing a sleeveless green sweatshirt inside out that had brown and black stains on it.

"These boys are young but they're able bodied," Buck shouted.

The man took a quick look up at Roy and Willy then returned his attention to the nets.

"Too young," he said. "A shrimp boat ain't no place for clean cut kids. Only lowlifes work shrimpers. Alkys, criminals, cut-throats, perverts. Nothin' to do but haul, mend, swill bad hooch like the devil's slaves and bugger each other."

"Maybe this isn't such a good idea, Unk," said Roy.

Two weeks later he and Willy were watching the TV news when a picture of the shrimp boat captain Buck had talked to came on the screen followed by a female reporter standing on the dock under the Bolívar Bridge.

"Albert Matanzas," said the reporter, "captain and owner of a shrimp boat out of Tampa, was discovered by the Coast Guard drifting in Tampa Bay close to death tied with a rope to the wheel of his boat with stab wounds in his left arm and shoulder and a bullet wound in his right leg. Two men were lying dead from gunshots on the deck. According to a statement Captain Matanzas gave to the Coast Guard, a third man was lost overboard in the Gulf after being shot by one of the dead men. It has not yet been determined what caused the dispute among the men. Matanzas remains in critical condition in Tampa General Hospital."

"Let's not ask your uncle if he has any more ideas," said Willy.

LEARNING THE GAME

"Hey, kid, what you think? We take this car, sell it, make big money."

Roy was waiting for his mother in her Buick Roadmaster convertible while she was inside her boyfriend Irwin's building on Clinton Street. Roy was six years old. It was mid-July but the late morning air was still cool and the car's top was up. His mother had said she'd be back in a couple of minutes, just long enough for her to pick up a few things from Irwin. His company manufactured women's undergarments: slips, panties, girdles, brassieres and hosiery. He owned a factory in Jackson, Mississippi, where the goods were made, and the building on Clinton Street in Chicago, where the design and shipping departments were located.

The small, brown man peered into the car. He had thick eyebrows and a thin mustache and was wearing a Panama hat.

"We get the money, go to Puerto Rico. I am from there, have many friends. We get the money, we are rico there, muy rico."

Roy's mother had left her keys dangling from the ignition. Roy, who was in the back seat, saw them and crawled into the front seat and took out the keys. Irwin's building was on the south side, neighbored by factories and meatpacking plants, all brown and gray brick buildings.

"What you say, chico? We go, huh?"

"No," Roy said. "This is my mother's car, she needs it."

"She rich. She get a new one."

"My father will shoot you."

Roy's mother came out of Irwin's building carrying two bags. The small, brown man walked away.

"It took a little longer than I thought it would, Roy. Were you worried?"

"No, Mom."

She put the bags on the back seat.

"You stay up front with me," she said.

"Did you see that little guy in the straw hat?"

His mother slid in behind the steering wheel.

'Where are my keys?"

Roy handed them to her.

"They were in the ignition. I took them out."

She adjusted the rear view mirror, then started the engine.

"What little guy, Roy?"

"A Puerto Rican man. He wanted me to steal the car with him."

"Don't be silly. He would have to be crazy to steal a car with a child in it."

"I told him Dad would shoot him if he did."

"You have such an imagination."

Roy's mother started driving.

"What if I told you that I'm thinking of marrying Irwin? After my divorce from your father is final, of course."

"He's too short for you, Mom."

"He is short, but he's very nice to me, and to you, too."

"Where are we going now?"

"I have to make one more quick stop, and then we can have lunch. Would you like to go to the Edgewater?"

"Have you ever been to Puerto Rico?"

"Yes, twice. Once with your father, and once with Johnny Sal-vavidas. Remember him, Roy? You were on his boat."

"Did Irwin ask you to marry him?"

"Not yet."

"Maybe he won't."

Roy's mother was a good driver. He always felt safe in the car with her. She drove for several blocks before Roy saw that she was crying.

"What's wrong, Mom? Are you upset?"

"Not really, Roy. Maybe you're right. Maybe Irwin doesn't want to get married."

"You could get anyone to marry you. You're beautiful and smart."

"And I have a good sense of humor. Don't I, Roy? We laugh a lot, don't we?"

"Yes, Mom. You're really funny."

"Hand me my dark glasses. They're in the glove compartment."

She put the glasses on.

"Did you stop crying?"

"Don't worry, Roy. I'm fine now."

They were driving next to the lake. The water was calm and many sailboats were out.

"What if I had been a girl?" Roy asked. "I mean, if you had a daughter instead of a son."

"What are you talking about?"

"Would you act different with her than you do with me?"

"What a strange question. I don't know, probably. Why did you ask me that?"

Roy watched the sailboats struggle to catch some wind. He didn't feel like talking to his mother any more.

THE FIFTH ANGEL

Roy fell asleep while he was watching a movie on TV about a twelve year old boy who's living in an isolated mountain cabin with his parents. His father is a failed writer, a novelist, and he's sickly; he should be living in a better climate, not in a snowbound redoubt with a wife who doesn't love him and a child who is not really his own. The boy's real father is the sick man's brother who the boy thinks is his uncle, a bank robber who shows up at the mountain retreat during a blizzard with a bullet wound in one leg, accompanied by two cohorts, a third having been captured during the getaway wherein two cops were killed. The bank robber is the boy's mother's old boyfriend; his brother married her to give the boy a home and a family. She's still in love with the bad brother, who intends to escape the manhunt by hiking over a supposedly impassable mountain trail. There's also a bleach blonde floozy, a warbler who can't carry a tune, who's hung up on the bank robber, as well as a handyman who lusts after the boy's mother and begs her to let him take her away from the invalid novelist. The boy is the hero, the only one who can lead the criminals over the dangerous pass.

Roy woke up just as the movie was ending. He was ten, two years younger than the intrepid boy, and he wondered if, given a similar circumstance, he would behave as bravely. His own mother had married her third husband a few months before, but

Roy knew it wouldn't last. They were fighting all the time and Roy did not want to continue living with them. He loved his mother but she was constantly on the verge of a nervous breakdown; Roy had overheard her talking on the telephone to his grandmother telling her she needed to be hospitalized or sent to a sanitarium, somewhere she could rest. Otherwise, his mother said, something terrible might happen. Roy figured this meant one of three things: that she would kill herself or her husband, or that her husband would kill her.

Roy didn't care about his stepfather. The best solution, Roy thought, would be for him to go away, to admit the marriage had been a mistake and leave Roy and his mother alone. It was a week before Christmas and snow was falling. Roy put on his parka and galoshes and went out the back door. He decided that if his mother and her husband did not separate, he would be the one to go. It was five o'clock in the afternoon and there was no light left in the sky. Roy walked into the alley behind his house. He was standing still, letting the snow cover him, when he heard shots, four of them in rapid succession.

Teddy Anderson, a nephew of Roy's neighbors Sven and Inga Anderson, came into the alley from behind the Andersons' garage holding a gun, an automatic. Teddy saw Roy and waved to him with his hand holding the gun. Teddy was twenty years old, he had always been nice to Roy, but Roy knew that Teddy was often in trouble with the law and that his uncle and aunt were trying to straighten him out. Teddy fired a shot into a garbage can behind Johnny Murphy's house, then he fell down and stayed there. Roy went over to him and saw that in his other hand Teddy was holding a bottle of brandy. He had passed out. Roy took both the gun and the bottle out of Teddy's hands and put them on the ground just inside the passageway next to the Andersons' garage, then he went back and dragged Teddy by his left leg out of the middle of the alley and propped him up against the garage door, just in case a car came through and the driver couldn't see Teddy lying in the snow.

When he'd heard the shots, Roy thought they could possibly have come from inside his house. If his mother was dead, since his father had died two years before, a court would probably order him to live with his grandmother, which he did not want to do. In this circumstance he would just run away, get out of Chicago, hop a freight train or hitchhike west, to California or Arizona, somewhere warm, like the writer in the movie should have done.

He looked at Teddy Anderson leaned against the garage door, sound asleep. Roy was surprised nobody had come into the alley after hearing the shots. He did not feel guilty about being disappointed that neither his mother nor his stepfather had been murdered. Roy walked back into the passageway, picked up the automatic and put it into his coat pocket. He would hide the gun somewhere in his room until he really needed to use it.

A LONG DAY'S NIGHT IN THE NAKED CITY
(TAKE TWO)

Roy's father had a friend in Cicero, Illinois, named Momo Giocoforza whom Roy visited once in a while when he was in high
school. He died a few years later but in those days Momo hung
out at the Villa Schioppo, a restaurant on Cermak Road next
to the Western Electric Company plant. Momo was part owner
of Hawthorne Racetrack, which was on the boundary between
Cicero and Stickney. Roy could usually find him in a back booth
of the Villa talking to men who always looked like they were in
a hurry. Momo, on the other hand, not only never seemed to be
in a hurry, but he hardly moved except to put a fork or glass to
his mouth. Momo was a fat man, close to three hundred pounds,
with very small hands, fingers no bigger than a ten year old child's.
He rarely shook hands. Momo always seemed glad to see Roy and
have plenty of time to talk with him. He insisted that Roy eat
something and would order food for both of them. Roy guessed
that Momo never stopped eating.

From what little Momo shared with him about his relationship with Roy's father, Roy gathered that they had done business
together during and after Prohibition, and he never asked Momo
for details. Once afternoon when Roy and Momo were having
linguini with clam sauce and discussing the vicissitudes of the
Chicago Blackhawks, of whom Momo was an avid follower, a

short, wiry guy entered the Villa Schioppo and came over to their table and held out to Momo a white envelope.

"It's all there," the man said. "I'm t'rough wid it."

Momo did not reach for the envelope so the man put it down on the table.

"Siddown," said Momo. "Have some linguini."

"Thanks, Mr. Giocoforza, but I can't. I got my cab outside. I'm workin'."

The man shifted his weight from foot to foot and looked nervously around the restaurant. He was about thirty-five years old, five-nine or ten, ordinary features. His eyes were so small Roy could not tell what color they were.

"So we're up to date now, right?" he said.

Momo barely nodded and said, "If you say so, Brian. I'm always here for you."

'No offense, Mr. Giocoforza, but I hope to Mother Mary I won't."

The man was jumpy, like he badly needed to take a piss.

"I'm goin'. Thanks a million, Mr. Giocoforza."

The man left and Momo picked up the envelope and slid it inside his coat pocket.

"Funny guy," Momo said to Roy. "He was a cop. He's moonlightin' one night, guardin' some buildin's onna Near North Side, and almost gets his eye shot out. Some fancy broad, a white girl, she's stoppin' cars—Mercedes, Jags, Cadillacs, expensive models—and tellin' the drivers she's got a flat tire or somethin'. As a driver's about to give her a lift, opens a door, a black guy dressed like a bum comes up behind her and drags her into an alley. Most drivers take off, but one hero gets out, chases the mugger.

"Now the broad's a real doll, dressed to the nines, and the hero's gonna save her, right? Thinkin' what she'll give in return. The black guy drops the woman when he sees the hero comin' to help her. The driver comforts the broad, takes her into his car, asks her where she wants to go. She pulls a pistol out of her purse, puts it to the hero's head, and the black guy jumps into the back seat, also wid a gun, tells the hero to drive. They go to his house or apartment, which they clean out the jewels and cash. Primo scam. Worked thirty-two times inna row until my pal here, the cop who's moonlightin' in order to save money for his weddin', spots the pair in the act.

"The cop attempts to pull the black guy out of this Mercedes, doesn't figure he an' the broad are workin' together, an' she plugs Brian point blank in the skull. Brian's lyin' onna sidewalk next to the car and the bum tumbles out right on toppa him. Brian's bleedin' all over but takes out his own piece and shoots the black guy, then passes out. When he wakes up, Brian's inna hospital wid his eye bandaged. He's barely alive an' doctors tell him maybe he won't lose the eye. The black bum's dead, the broad got away clean.

"While Brian's inna hospital, his girl never comes to see him. She thinks he's gonna die. He's already given her ten, fourteen thousand for the weddin'. She's why he was workin' a second job inna first place, right? So while he's inna hospital fightin' to recover, she runs off wid another joker. By the time Brian's on the street again he's in deep shit. The police department insurance policy won't cover him 'cause he was off duty workin' for a private security firm, and they don't cover part-timers. So he comes to me, knows a guy knows me. Brian's suin' the insurance company, the owner of the buildin' he was guardin' that night, the police department, everybody he can think of, payin' some ambulance chaser to do it. On toppa that he's afraid to go see the girl threw him over 'cause he'd put six inna her. Now he's pushin' a hack tryna get back on his feet. I give him a good deal, plenya time to pay me back, right? Why not? Your dad, he helped out plenya guys."

THE RELIGIOUS EXPERIENCE

"I was in Brazil, with Antonio. When we flew into Rio the plane passed over the big statue of Christ on top of Corcovado and for the entire time I was there I couldn't get that out of my head. The statue, I mean, the way it commanded everything below, in every direction. When I had an orgasm the image of Jesus on the mountaintop was in my mind, like I was coming with Him, not Antonio."

"How old were you?"

"Twenty-five. Rudy and I were separated and when Antonio invited me to go with him to Brazil, I just said yes, without thinking. I left Roy with my mother in Miami and we flew from there."

"And that was the first time?"

"Uh huh, and it didn't happen again—not with Antonio, anyway. I only saw him two or three times after we got back to Chicago."

Roy's mother and her friend Kay were standing in the lobby of the Oriental Theater. Kay was smoking a cigarette. Her husband, Harvey, and Kitty's son, Roy, who was eight years old, were inside the theater watching the last few minutes of *The Proud Ones*, a western starring Robert Ryan as a sheriff in a Kansas town who's going blind.

"Do you think if I went to Brazil I could have an orgasm with Harvey?"

The two women laughed and Kitty said, "Maybe you should go with Antonio."

"Is he my type?"

"He looks like Chico, the Mexican gunfighter in the movie, only taller. But Antonio was only an instrument of the Son of God."

"You should do a commercial for the Catholic Church, Kitty, standing in a mink coat, saying, 'Jesus made me come.' Or, 'I came for Christ.'"

"I'm sure the nuns believe it when they masturbate."

"I thought they weren't allowed to."

People began coming out of the theater.

"Mom, you missed the best part. The sheriff can't see but he uses his hearing to figure out where the bad guy is and shoots him down, anyway."

Kay's husband lit a cigarette and watched the crowd leaving.

"See anything you like?" Kay asked.

"The movie was okay. The kid liked it."

"I mean the women in the lobby."

"Lay off, Kay."

"Kitty was just telling me about the time she went to Brazil."

"I remember when you went there, Mom. You brought me back a little statue of Jesus Christ standing on the top of a mountain."

"Did you have fun there, Kitty?" Harvey asked.

"She certainly did," said Kay. "She even had a religious experience."

"What kind of religious experience?"

"Kay's just being silly."

"No, really. She had an epiphany."

"What's that?" asked Roy.

"It's when you see God," said Kay, "or you feel Him inside you."

"Do you have to be a Catholic to have one?"

"No, Roy," Kay said, "but it probably helps."

"You're a godsend, Rudy. Thanks for helping me out. I won't forget it."

"I'm the one doesn't forget."

"I know, I know. You didn't have to do this."

Rudy turned around and entered Lake Shore Liquors. His partners in the store, Earl LaDuke, who was Rudy's uncle, and Dick Mooney, were waiting for him. Moe Herman, to whom Rudy had just handed a double sawbuck, went on his way. Rudy never loaned money to anyone; either he gave someone what he or she needed or refused without providing an explanation. All anyone in dire straits wants to hear is yes or no. If he was paid back, so much the better, but there never was a reason to count on it.

Earl and Dick were seated at a card table in the basement. Rudy's uncle was smoking a cigar with his eyes closed, and Dick was scrutinizing the previous day's results at Sportsman's Park. Rudy sat down and poured himself a finger of Jameson's from a bottle on the table.

"Good afternoon, Rudy. How's Kitty?"

"Fine, Earl."

"You'll tell her I asked."

Dick put down the paper and took off his glasses.

"Nothing yet," he said.

"If it's not here by tonight, I'll call. Not before then."

Earl LaDuke opened his eyes and stood up. He was a big, ungainly man. Rudy wondered how he could have outrun the hussars in the old country when his name was Sackgasse.

"I'll be home. Your Aunt Sofia would like it if you and Kitty came for dinner."

"We will, Uncle Earl. Not tonight, but soon. Kiss her for me."

"I can still kiss her for myself, I want to. I can still do that."

Earl walked slowly up the stairs.

"You're not worried?" Dick asked.

"The roads are icy."

"Emily wants to leave Chicago. Her sister's in Atlanta."

"Earl and I can cover your share."

Dick was thirty-two, ten years younger than Rudy and twenty-seven years younger than Earl LaDuke. He had bought into Lake Shore five years before and his third was worth twice as much now.

"I could be your man down there."

"Atlanta belongs to Lozano."

There were footsteps on the stairs. The two men looked up and saw Lola Wilson, a dancer from the Club Alabam next door, coming down. She was wearing a fur coat over her rehearsal costume. When the front of the coat swung to either side, they could see her legs. Lola descended cautiously, placing her high heels delicately on each of the rickety wooden steps. She came over and stood behind the chair on which Rudy's uncle had been sitting.

Dick got up, said, "Hello, Lola. See you later, Rudy," and started up the stairs.

Lola sat down, took out a crumpled pack of Camels and a book of matches from a pocket of her coat, then changed her mind and replaced them in the pocket.

"You don't like it that I smoke. Sometimes I forget. Kitty doesn't smoke, does she?"

"No, she doesn't."

"I saw Roy down here with her the other day. He's getting big. He must be about ten now."

"Eight. What can I do for you, Lola?"

Lola had a sharply upturned nose, rose-colored full lips, dark brown swampy eyes and blonde hair translucent at the ends. Her face fascinated most men and women, especially women, very few of whom were gifted with such dramatically contrasting features that so exquisitely combined. Lola's teeth were crooked and tobacco-stained; they embarrassed her so when she smiled she determinedly pressed her lips together. Before he married Kitty, when Lola was eighteen, fresh off the bus from West Virginia, Rudy had offered to pay to have her teeth straightened but she had demurred, and then it was too late.

"You'll hate me," she said.

"What is it?"

"I picked up a dose. Can you give me a shot?"

Rudy got up, walked to the rear of the room, opened the door of a small refrigerator and took out a little round bottle. He opened a drawer in a cabinet next to the refrigerator and removed a hypodermic syringe and a thin packet containing needles, one of which he shook out and fitted to the syringe, then drew fluid from the bottle before replacing it in the refrigerator. Rudy picked up a brown bottle, took a cotton ball from a box and walked back to the table.

Lola stood, turned her back to Rudy and held one side of the fur coat away from her body. Rudy sat down, daubed the exposed part of her left buttock with the piece of cotton he'd soaked in alcohol from the brown bottle, then inserted the needle into the sanitized spot and injected the penicillin, after which he again brushed the spot with the cotton ball before standing up and walking back to a sink next to the cabinet and placing the items he had employed into it.

"How long were you in medical school, Rudy?"

"A year and a half. I've told you this. When they rolled the cadaver in, they rolled me out. After that I transferred to pharmacy school."

"Do I need a band-aid?"

"You'll be all right."

Lola sat down again, as did Rudy. She balanced herself carefully on her right buttock.

"Really, I don't know what I'd do if you weren't in my life."

"I thought you were going to marry Manny Shore."

"I can't go on dancing forever. I figured at least it would get me off my feet, but no. I realized it wasn't going to work. I haven't seen him in months. Weeks, anyway. Rudy, do you think I'm a trollop?"

"Where did you learn that word?"

"Monique said somebody called her one and I asked her what it meant. She didn't know exactly, so I looked it up. Did you think I was a trollop when we met?"

"You're not Monique. You have to take better care of yourself."

Lola stood up.

"I have to get back to rehearsal."

She leaned down and kissed Rudy behind his right ear.

"Am I still pretty? Not as pretty as your wife, I know, but tell me."

Rudy stood and looked into her murky eyes.

"Yes," he said, "you are."

Lola turned and walked up the stairs. When she reached the top step she paused and said, loud enough for him to hear, "I'm twenty-nine."

"Mr. Randolph is very nice, Rudy. He offered to let us use his house in the Bahamas any time we want."

"It's all right for you to be polite to Mr. Ruggiano, Kitty. Or anyone else, for that matter. Just keep your distance."

"Who's Mr. Ruggiano?"

"Ralph Randolph is the name he uses when it suits his purpose."

"What about Marshall Gottlieb?"

"What about him?"

"Is that his real name?"

"It was something else when his family came from Poland or Russia."

"Like yours."

Kitty stood up and put on her candy-striped terrycloth robe.

"I'm going to the room to call my mother and talk to Roy," she said, and walked around the pool into the hotel.

Kitty and Rudy were staying at El Rancho Vegas. Their son, Roy, who was almost three years old, was being looked after by his grandmother in Chicago. Luchino Benedetti came over and sat down in the chair Kitty had been using.

"Your wife is a real doll, Rudy," he said. "Everybody likes her, even the other wives."

"Thanks, Lucky. She's having a swell time. We both appreciate your hospitality. You keep a good house."

"Kitty got a lot to show, but she don't show it. She has class."

"She was raised right."

"Leave it to the sisters. How is your boy?"

"Growing up fast. He's back home with Kitty's mother."

"My Rocco joined the Air Force. He wants to be a pilot."

"I heard. I'm sure he'll do well."

"So, our thing with the Diamond brothers."

"All I know is, the goods are always on time, and they're always what Sam and Moses say they are."

"They move."

"If they didn't, Rugs would know."

"Did you hear about Sam's wife?"

"Dolores. A nice woman."

"She run off with Solly Banks's son, Victor."

"Run off? Where to?"

"New York. Sam's there now, it's why he ain't here. Rugs is afraid this will interfere with our business, and that can't happen."

"I'll talk to Moses."

"Do it now."

Kitty came back and Lucky jumped up.

"Hello, Kitty. I was just telling Rudy what a hit you are with everyone."

"Thank you, Lucky," she said, and sat down in the chair.

"See you at dinner," said Lucky, and walked away.

"Did you speak to Roy?"

"Yes, he's fine. The janitor found a dead rat in his fire truck and showed it to him. The tail was as long as Roy's arm."

"Did they bury the rat in the yard?"

"No, the janitor burned it in the furnace. Roy was about to take his nap. He told me to kiss his daddy for him."

Kitty kissed her husband on the cheek.

"And Rose?"

"I'm worried about her heart condition. She doesn't have the energy she used to."

"Has she seen Dr. Martell?"

"Unless he's operating, he comes to the house every evening to have a glass of wine."

"Your mother will be all right. Martell would leave his wife for her in a minute if Rose gave him some encouragement."

"My mother says he has a tax problem. He could lose his hospital."

Marshall Gottlieb and his wife, Sarah, came over.

"Come with me, Kitty," Sarah said. "We're going to have our fingernails and toenails done."

Kitty got up and went with her. Marshall sat down.

"Lucky told you?"

"About Sam Diamond? I told him I'll talk to Moses."

"Moses just called Mr. Randolph two minutes ago. His brother shot and killed Dolores and Victor Banks in their room at the Waldorf, then he phoned Moses to tell him what he'd done and that he was going to kill himself. Next thing, Moses hears a shot."

Arlene Silverman, Art and Edith Silverman's seventeen year old daughter, dove into the pool. Rudy and Marshall Gottlieb watched her swim.

"Arlene's a lovely girl, isn't she?" said Marshall. "How is it she has gorgeous blonde hair when neither of her parents do?"

"She's adopted," said Rudy.

"Oh yeah? I didn't know."

Arlene Silverman swam the length of the pool twice before Ralph Randolph helped her climb out.

"Lotsa times," Marshall said, "after you get what you want, you don't want it. That ever happen to you?"

IN DREAMS

Roy's grandfather was watching a baseball game on television when his grandson came home from school.

"What's on, Pops?" Roy asked.

"The White Sox are playing the Senators. Two outs in the ninth. Billy Pierce is pitching a perfect game."

Roy sat down on the floor next to his grandfather's chair. Ed Fitzgerald, Washington's catcher, was the last chance for them to break up the no-hitter.

"Fitzgerald bats left-handed," Roy said. "Since Pierce is a southpaw, shouldn't he just throw breaking balls?"

"He might hang one, Roy, but Pierce is crafty. He'd probably do better to start him off with a fastball high and outside, then go to the curve."

Fitzgerald lined one off the right field fence for a double.

"Pierce went with the fast ball, Pops."

"It caught too much of the plate. He should have gone away with it."

The game ended when the next batter made an out. Roy's grandfather turned off the set.

"Too bad," said Roy. "A pitcher doesn't get many chances to throw a perfect game."

"There have only been about twenty perfect games in the history of major league baseball. How was school, boy? What grade are you in now?"

"Fourth. I don't know, Pops. I think I learn more important things talking to you and some other people. I like it when you tell me stories about your life."

"Don't ignore dreams, Roy. You can learn a lot from them."

"I don't always remember what I dream."

"Write them down as soon as you wake up, even if you're groggy and only half awake. For me, the most interesting dreams are the ones in which people who have died appear."

"Like who?"

"I recently had a dream about a very old, close friend of mine who died about twelve or thirteen years ago, before you were born. His name was Warren Winslow. In my dream someone told me he heard that Warren was living in Chicago in the house of a person I didn't know. He gave me the address so I went there and found Warren, looking much as he had when both of us were younger. He was calm, sitting on a couch with a blanket across his legs. I asked him how this could have happened, how he had recovered, why he hadn't told me and let me know he was here in Chicago."

"What did he say?"

"He said that he had died but come back to life and was rather embarrassed to have done so. He asked the doctors in the hospital where he had been treated not to tell anyone, and he left everything he owned and came to stay with a fellow he did not know very well who was willing to keep his existence and whereabouts a secret."

"Why?"

"Warren himself was not entirely certain other than he felt satisfied that at the time of his death he was not displeased by the state of his affairs and his relations with those closest to him. I told him I had missed him and Warren said he had always valued our friendship highly. Now that I knew where he was, Warren told me, I could visit him if I chose to, but warned me that he didn't know how much longer he would be there. It wasn't so much that his attitude was one of indifference—at least I didn't take it that way—so much as his having moved on from the past."

"What did you do?"

"I left the house, then I woke up. This is the way the dead visit us, Roy, in dreams. It's the only way we can be with them again."

"That's pretty spooky, Pops. See, this is the kind of stuff they don't teach us in school."

LUCKY

"You sure the coal man's comin' this mornin'?"

"He usually comes around nine or ten every other Saturday during the winter. Depends on how many deliveries he has."

Roy and his friend Johnny Murphy were standing in the alley behind Roy's house waiting for the coal truck to arrive. Two feet of snow had fallen during the night, then the temperature had dropped, so the ground was covered by a frozen crust. The boys, who were both eight years old, liked to slide down the coal chute into the pile in front of the furnace in the basement. The best time to do it was on delivery day, when the pile was highest.

"I'm freezin'," said Johnny. "I shoulda worn two pairs of socks."

It was almost ten o'clock when they heard and then saw the big red Peterson Coal truck turn into the alley. The truck crunched ahead and skidded to a stop in front of Roy's garage. Alfonso Rivero, the driver, climbed down from the cab and tromped over to where Roy and Johnny were standing. Alfonso was a short, stocky man in his mid-forties. He was wearing a black knit hat pulled down over his ears, a navy blue tanker jacket and steel-toed work boots. An unfiltered Camel hung from his lips.

"You waiting go slide?" he said.

"Hi, Alfonso," said Roy. "Yeah, I thought you might be late because of the snow and ice."

"We been out here since nine," said Johnny Murphy.

"I hate the nieve," Alfonso said. "In Mexico, no hay snow and ices, except in los montañas."

"Why do you live in Chicago?" asked Johnny.

"We don't have no work in Mexico, also."

Roy and Johnny watched Alfonso take down a wheelbarrow mounted on the back of the truck and set it on the ground, then open the two rear doors and hoist himself inside. He pulled a thick glove from each of his side pockets, put them on, picked a shovel out of the coal pile and began shoveling it down into the wheelbarrow. When the barrow was full, he leaned down holding the shovel.

"Take la pala, chico," he said to Roy.

Roy took it and the deliveryman jumped down. Roy handed Alfonso the shovel. He stuck it into the pile of coal in the wheelbarrow and wheeled it through the passageway leading to Roy's backyard. The boys followed Alfonso, who stopped in front of a pale blue door at the rear of the building, undid the latch on the door and swung it open. He shoveled most of the contents of the wheelbarrow down the chute and dumped in the rest, then headed back to the truck for another load.

After six trips back and forth, Alfonso said to the boys, "Es todo, muchachos. Okay now for deslizamiento."

"Muchas gracias, Alfonso," said Roy.

"Yeah, mucho," said Johnny.

Roy went first, sliding all the way down and landing in front of the furnace. As soon as he got up, Johnny did the same. They went out the basement door and ran up the steps into the yard.

"Once more, Alfonso!" Roy shouted.

"Si, uno mas," said the deliveryman, and lit up a fresh cigarette.

After the boys emerged from the basement, Alfonso closed the door to the chute, latched it, and pushed the wheelbarrow back into the alley. Roy and Johnny trailed him and watched as he tossed in his shovel, closed the doors and re-attached the wheelbarrow.

"See you dos semanas, amigos," Alfonso said, then climbed into the cab, started the engine and drove slowly away down the alley.

Roy and Johnny's faces were covered with coal dust, as were their hands and clothes. They picked up clean snow, washed their faces and hands with it and rubbed it on their coats and pants.

"I wouldn't mind havin' Alfonso's job," said Johnny. "You get to drive a big truck and stand around smokin' cigarettes in people's yards."

"Alfonso's a good guy," said Roy. "He probably lets any kid who wants to slide down the piles."

"It don't seem so cold now," Johnny said. "You hear about Cunningham's mother?"

"No. What about her?"

"She died yesterday."

"Tommy didn't say anything about her being sick."

"My father says she committed suicide. It's a mortal sin, so now she can't get into heaven."

"Maybe it was an accident."

"My father says she ate a bullet."

"What's that mean?"

"Shot herself in the mouth. She's probably already in hell."

"Don't say that to Cunningham."

"My mother said she thinks Tommy's father pulled the trigger."

"Why would he murder her?"

"When husbands and wives are arguin' they're always sayin' how they're gonna kill each other. I hate hearin' it when my parents fight. You're lucky you only got a mother."

DANGER IN THE AIR

Roy liked to fly with his mother. Most of the time they drove between Key West or Miami, Florida, and Chicago, the places in which they lived; but if they needed to be somewhere in a hurry, they took an airplane. Roy's mother always dressed well when they flew, and she made sure Roy did, too.

"You never know who you might meet in an airport or on a plane," she told him, "so it's important to look your best."

"Even a little boy?"

"Of course, Roy. You're with me. I'm so proud of you. You're a great traveler."

"Thanks, Mom. I'm proud of you, too."

One afternoon when they were flying from Miami to New Orleans to see Roy's mother's boyfriend Johnny Salvavidas, their plane ran into a big storm and lightning hit both wings. The plane tilted to the right, then to the left, like Walcott taking a combination from Marciano, only the airplane didn't go down.

"We're really getting knocked around, Roy. Better keep your head down in case things start flying out of the overhead compartments."

"I want to look out the window, Mom. I have a book about lightning, remember? The worst thing that can happen is if the fuel tank gets hit, then the plane could explode. Also, lightning can make holes in the wings and pieces of them can fall off. If it strikes the nose, the pilot could lose control and even be blinded. And during thunderstorms ball lightning can enter an airplane and roll down the aisle. That's pretty rare, though, and the fireball burns out fast and leaves a kind of smoky mist in the air. Some scientists even believe ball lightning might come from flying saucers."

"Don't be silly, Roy. There's no such things as flying saucers. That's just in movies and comic books."

When the plane landed at the airport in New Orleans, Johnny Salvavidas was there to meet it. He asked Roy's mother if it had been a good flight.

"It was horrendous," she told him. "We ran into a terrible thunderstorm and there was a lot of turbulence. My stomach is still upset."

"What about it, Roy? Was the storm as bad as your mother says?"

"Lightning hit the wings," Roy said. "We could have gotten knocked out of the sky, but we weren't."

Johnny smiled and said, "That can't happen."

He smoothed back both sides of his hair with his hands. His hair was black and shiny and fit tightly to his scalp like a bathing cap. He took Roy's mother's right arm and they walked together toward the terminal to pick up her suitcases.

The sun was going down and the sky was turning redder. What did Johnny Salvavidas know? There was a kind of lightning that moved across rather than up and down called spider or creepy-crawly lightning that can reverse itself and probably bring down a spaceship. Roy watched his mother and Johnny enter the terminal. He wanted to get back on an airplane.

CHILD'S PLAY

The two Greek brothers, Nick and Peter, had settled in Jackson, Mississippi, in 1935, three years after they emigrated with their parents from Patnos. Their father, Constantin, had worked in a grocery store for a Jewish family in New York City, where the immigrants had landed; but when the Great Depression cost Constantin his job, rather than join a bread line he used the few dollars he had saved to move his family south, where, he'd been told, it was cheaper to live. The Jewish grocers had a cousin who traveled in a wagon throughout Mississippi peddling household goods who apparently made a decent living, so Constantin informed his wife and sons, ages six and nine, to take only what they could comfortably carry, and they entrained to another, quite different, country.

In Jackson, the state capital, Constantin and his wife, Josefa, found part-time employment as night cleaners in government buildings, then Constantin got a job scrubbing down a diner frequented by local businessmen and politicians. After six months, he was hired on as a waiter, and within a year the owner died. With the assistance of several of the patrons, Constantin bought the diner, which he renamed The Athens Café. Josefa and their sons worked with him and soon The Athens was the most popular restaurant in town. After their parents died, Nick and Peter took over.

During the year or so that Roy's mother had a boyfriend named Boris Klueber, who owned a girdle factory on the outskirts of Jackson, they often accompanied him when he traveled there from his headquarters in Chicago. Roy and his mother always stayed in the Heidelberg Hotel, as did Boris. The Heidelberg was the best hotel in Jackson, located only a few blocks from The Athens Café. This was in 1955, when Roy was eight years old.

Negroes were not allowed to eat in the diner, but all of the kitchen workers, including the cooks, were black. To get to the toilets, which were accessible only by a steep flight of stairs, customers were required to go through the kitchen. It was in this way that Roy became friendly with the employees. He was friendly, too, of course, with the owners, who enjoyed showing him photographs they took in Greece on their annual vacations. Neither of the brothers ever married, but Roy's mother told him that according to Boris both of the brothers kept Negro mistresses.

"What's a mistress?" Roy asked her.

"Women who aren't married to the men who support them."

"Why don't they marry them?"

"Well, in Mississippi, it's against the law for white and black men and women to marry each other. Don't repeat what I'm telling you, Roy, especially to Nick and Peter. Promise?"

"I promise."

"It's a sensitive issue in the South."

"Can Negroes and whites get married to each other in Chicago?"

"Yes, Roy. Laws are often different in different states. In Mississippi, and some other southern states, a white man can get arrested for dating a black woman; and a black man can be put in prison or even murdered for being in the company of a white woman. I know this doesn't make sense, but that's the way it is. As long as we're here we have to respect their laws."

"What if you went on a date with a Negro man? Would you be arrested and the man murdered or thrown in jail?"

"Let's not talk about this any more, Roy. I shouldn't have told you about Nick and Peter. And don't mention it to Boris. Promise?"

"I already did."

A couple of days later, while Roy was cutting through the kitchen of The Athens Café to use the toilet, one of the cooks, Emmanuel, who was taking a cigarette break by the back door, said to him, "How you doin' today, little man? You enjoyin' yourself?"

"Sort of. There's not much for me to do. I don't have anyone to play with."

"I got a boy about your age. His name's John Daniel."

"Can I meet him?"

Emmanuel removed his wallet from one of his back pockets, took out a photograph and handed it to Roy.

"That's John Daniel, that's my son."

"He's white," said Roy, "like me."

"That's on account of his mama is white. He's got her colorin'."

"My mother says white and black people can't get married to each other in Mississippi."

"That's right. John Daniel's mama and I ain't married, not to each other. I don't get to see him except his mama sneak me a walk by."

"There's a Negro boy in Chicago I play with. His name's Henry Cherokee, and he's part Indian."

"Me, too. My grandmama on my daddy's side is half Choctaw."

Roy returned the photo of John Daniel to Emmanuel, which he replaced in his wallet.

"Gotta get back to work," he said, and tossed his cigarette butt into the street.

That evening Roy and his mother were having dinner with Boris in the dining room of the Heidelberg Hotel when Boris whispered to her, "See that waiter there? The one who looks like Duke Ellington."

Roy's mother looked at the waiter, who, like the other waiters, was wearing a tuxedo.

"He's quite handsome," she said.

"He's Mrs. Van Nostrand's back door man."

"Sshh. Don't talk that way around Roy. Why do you have your factory here, Boris? I don't like Jackson."

"Manufacturing's cheap. No unions, no taxes. It would cost me four times as much to have a plant in Chicago like I have here."

Roy watched the waiter Boris had said resembled Duke Ellington as he served an old white man and an old white woman at another table.

"Mom," he said, "the next time we come here, could we bring Henry Cherokee with us?"

THE MESSAGE

Roy was alone in the hotel room he shared with his mother when the telephone rang. It was ten to four in the morning and Roy was less than half awake, watching *Journey into Fear* on TV. He'd fallen asleep on and off during the movie, and when the telephone rang Roy looked first at the television and saw Orson Welles, wearing a gigantic military overcoat with what looked like dead, furry animals for lapels and a big fur hat littered with snow. The picture was tilted and for a moment Roy thought that he had fallen off the bed, then he realized it was the camera angled for effect.

"Kitty, that you?"

"No. She's not here, I don't think."

"Who's this?"

"Her son."

"She's got a kid? How old are you?"

"Seven. Six and a half, really."

"Your mother didn't tell me she had a kid. How many more kids she have?"

"None."

"What's your name?"

"Roy."

"You sure she's not there?"

"No. Yeah, I'm sure."

"Know where she is?"

"She went out with some friends, around ten o'clock."

"It's almost four now. She was supposed to meet me at one. Said she maybe would, anyway."

"Do you want to leave a message?"

"Yeah, okay. Dimitri, tell her. If she comes in, I'll be in the bar at the Roosevelt Hotel until five."

"All right."

"She leaves you alone this time of night, in the room?"

Orson Welles was growling at someone, a smaller man who kept his head down. The picture was lopsided, as if the camera had been kicked over and it was lying on the floor but still rolling.

"Kid, she leaves you by yourself?"

"I'm okay."

"She's kind of a kook, your mother. You know that?"

Orson Welles did not take off his coat even though he was in an office.

"Go back to sleep, kid. Sorry I woke you up."

Roy hung up the phone. He and his mother had been in this city for a week and Roy was anxious to return to Key West, where they lived in a hotel located at the confluence of the Gulf of Mexico and the Atlantic Ocean. A beautiful, dark-haired woman was on the screen now but she kept turning her head away from the camera so Roy could not see all of her face. She looked Cuban, or Indian.

When Roy woke up again, the television was off and his mother was asleep in the other bed. He looked at the clock: it was just past ten. The heavy drapes were drawn so even though the sun was up the light in the room was very dim. Roy's mother always hung the Do Not Disturb sign on the outside doorknob. She was wearing a blindfold. Roy lay listening to her breathe, whistling a little through her nose as she exhaled.

What was the name of the man who had called? When she woke up, Roy would tell his mother that a general or a colonel with a strange accent had called from a foreign country. Roy could not remember his name, only that the man had said it was snowing where he was calling from.

RIVER WOODS

Roy's father drove as if his powder blue Cadillac were the only car on the road. In the fall of 1953 there wasn't much traffic between Chicago and the western suburb of River Woods, where they were headed. It was mid-October, Roy's favorite time of the year. Sunlight slithered through the trees and the air was comfortably cool; in a month they would have to keep the car windows closed and the heater on.

"Who are we going to see, Dad?"

"A business associate of mine, Jocko Mosca. He has a classy layout in River Woods."

"Does he have kids?"

"Two sons, much older than you. They don't live here."

"Did you tell him tomorrow's my birthday?"

"You can tell him."

"Jocko is a funny name."

"It's short for Giacomo. He was born in Sicily, which is an island off the heel of Italy."

The houses they passed were set far back from the road. Most of them had long, winding driveways leading to buildings you couldn't see from a car, and some were behind iron fences with spikes on the top. Jocko Mosca's house had an iron fence in front of it but the gates were open. Roy's father drove in and stopped next to the house. Just as he and Roy got out of the car, a man came out and shook hands with Roy's father.

"Rudy, good to see you," he said. "This is your boy?"

"Hello, Lou. Roy, this is Lou Napoli. He works with Mr. Mosca."

Lou Napoli was not a large man but he had very big hands. He shook hands with Roy and smiled at him.

"You're fortunate to have a son, Rudy. And one handsome enough to be Italian. Quanti anni ha?" he asked Roy.

"He wants to know how old you are," said Roy's father.

"I'll be seven tomorrow."

"A lucky number," said Lou. "Let's go in."

They descended three steps into an enormous living room. The ceiling was very high with little sparkling lights in it. The walls were made of stone. There were five or six couches, several armchairs, lots of tables and lamps and a stone fireplace that ran nearly the entire length of one wall. A swimming pool snaked under a glass door into the rear of the room.

"I've never seen a swimming pool in a living room before," Roy said.

"This is only part of the pool," said Lou. "The rest of it is outside, on the other side of that glass door. It's heated. You want to take a dip?"

"I didn't bring a bathing suit."

"If you want to go in, let me know and we'll find you one. I'll tell Jocko you're here."

"Pretty swank, isn't it, son?"

"Jocko must be really rich."

"Call him Mr. Mosca. Yes, he's done well for himself. When his family came to America, from Sicily, they had nothing."

"Your parents didn't have anything when they came to America, either, Dad, and you were ten years old. How old was Mr. Mosca when his family came?"

"Probably about the same age I was. None of that matters now. We're Americans."

"Jocko is here," announced Lou Napoli.

Jocko Mosca was wearing a dark gray suit, a light blue shirt and a black tie. He was tall, had a big nose and full head of silver hair. He entered the room from a door behind a bend in the pool. Roy noticed that there was no knob on the door. Roy's father waited for Jocko to walk over to him. They embraced, then shook hands, each man using both of their hands.

"It's good of you to come all the way out here, Rudy," Jocko said.

"We enjoyed the drive. This is my son, Roy."

Jocko Mosca leaned down as he shook hands with Roy. His nose was covered with small holes and tiny red bumps.

"Benvenuto, Roy. That means welcome in Italian."

"I know. Angelo taught me some Italian words."

"Who is Angelo?"

"He's an organ grinder. He has a monkey named Dopo. They come into my dad's store and have coffee and Dopo dunks doughnuts in the cup with me. Dopo means after."

Jocko stood up straight and said, "Rudy, you didn't tell me your boy's a paesan'."

They laughed, then Jocko said to Roy, "I hope you'll be comfortable in here while your father and I go into another room to talk."

"I'll be okay, Mr. Mosca."

"Call me Jocko. We're paesanos, after all."

The two men left the room and Roy sat down on a couch. A pretty young woman with long black hair, wearing a maid's uniform, came in carrying a tray, which she set down on a low table.

"This is a ham sandwich, sweet pickles and a Coca-Cola for

you," she said. "If you need something, press that button on the wall behind you."

Roy felt sleepy, so he lay down and closed his eyes. When he reopened them, Lou Napoli was standing in front of him, holding a cake with eight candles on it.

"Did you have a nice nap, Roy?" he asked.

Jocko Mosca and Roy's father were there, as was the maid.

"He must have been tired from the drive," said Roy's father. "We got up very early today."

Lou passed the cake to the maid, who put it on a table and lit the candles. Lou, the maid, Jocko and Roy's father sang "Happy Birthday", then Lou said, "Make a wish and blow out the candles. The eighth one is for good luck."

Roy silently wished that his father would come back to live with him and his mother. He blew out all of the candles with one try.

Later, while his father was putting what was left of the cake, which the maid had put into a blue box, in the trunk of the Cadillac, Jocko Mosca handed Roy a little white card.

"This is my telephone number, Roy," he said. "If you ever have a problem, or anything you want to talk about, call me. Keep the card in a safe place, keep it for yourself. Don't show it to anyone."

"Can I show it to my dad?"

"He knows the number."

Roy's father started the car. Roy and Jocko shook hands, then Jocko opened the front passenger side door for him.

"Remember, Roy, I'm here for you, even just to talk. I like to talk."

Jocko closed the door and waved. He and Lou Napoli watched as Roy's father navigated the driveway.

"You all right, son? Wasn't it a nice surprise that they had a cake for you?"

"Do you want to know my wish?"

"No. You should keep what you wish for to yourself. Remember that you can't depend only on wishing for something to come true. It will always be up to you to make it happen."

"Always?"

"Always."

The gate in front of one of the houses had a metal sculpture of a fire-breathing dragon's head on it.

"River Woods is a beautiful place, isn't it, Roy? Would you rather live out here or in the city?"

"I don't know, Dad. I like when we're driving and we're not anywhere yet."

"So do I, son. Maybe, now that you're older, we're beginning to think alike."

THE HISTORY AND PROOF OF THE
SPOTS ON THE SUN

Roy accompanied his friend Frank to see a foreign movie Frank wanted to see at a little theater near The Loop.

"What language is it in?" Roy asked him.

"French. It'll have the translation in English on the bottom of the screen, but the words are only on for a few seconds so most of the time I can't finish reading it."

"I know. My mother likes to see foreign movies. I used to go with her when I was younger."

Both of the boys were thirteen years old. They had been close friends since the age of nine. Frank lived with his mother and two older brothers in a tenement on the same block as Roy and his mother. Frank's mother worked selling vacuum cleaners door to door. She slept in a bed that folded down from a wall in their livingroom, and the three boys shared a room with two beds in it. Roy and his mother lived in a larger apartment that she had inherited from one of her grandfathers. She worked as a receptionist in a hospital. Both Roy and Frank's fathers were dead, Frank's from a heart attack when Frank was seven, and Roy's from cancer when Roy was ten. Roy was an only child, his mother had been married and divorced twice; Frank's mother remained a widow.

Once Roy had heard her say to Frank and his brothers, "Men are like spots on the sun. Who knows what they are or how they got there? A woman can't even be sure they'll still be there the next day."

"But Ma," Frank's oldest brother, Ronnie, who was sixteen, said, "we'll all be men soon."

"I suppose you'll take care of me when I'm old, won't you?" she asked.

"Of course we will," answered Arnie, the middle brother.

"Proof! I don't have any proof!" their mother shouted, then put on a coat, picked up her purse and left the apartment.

The theater was only half full. Roy and Frank were the youngest people there. The movie's title was *Cela ne fait rien* (*It Makes No Difference*). The actors did not do anything much except talk and smoke cigarettes, and at the very end a woman took off her clothes, walked into the ocean and disappeared.

When they were back outside, Roy asked Frank, "Why did you want to see that movie?"

"My brother Ronnie's girlfriend, Rhonda, said her cousin, Lisa, who's studying to be an actress, told her it was smart and sexy."

"The woman who drowned herself kept her back to the camera," Roy said, "so we didn't even get to see her tits. In most of the foreign movies my mother took me to the women always showed their tits."

"Yeah, that was disappointing," said Frank, "and the translation went by so fast I couldn't get it all."

"There was too much talking," Roy said, "but the part where the boy found a gun under his mother's pillow was interesting."

"I wouldn't have put it back," Frank said. "I thought he should have shot her boyfriend when the guy hit her."

"After the guy walked out and she was lying on the floor, did you catch what she said to her son?"

"Yes," said Frank, "the boy asked why he'd hit her and she said, 'Because he loves me.' I would've gone into her bedroom, gotten the gun and run after the guy and plugged him. All she did was put a cigarette in her mouth and tell the boy to get a match and light it."

It was already dark and beginning to snow when Roy and Frank came out of the movie theater, but they walked slowly anyway. The top of the head of the statue in front of Our Lady of Insufferable Insolence was white. As Roy and Frank passed the church Roy remembered his grandmother Rose telling him that Saint Pantera had been born in Africa but the archdiocese would not allow her face and hands to be painted black.

"Do you think the kid was better off after his mother committed suicide?" Roy asked.

"I don't know. We never got to see his father, who lived in a different country. Switzerland, someone said. Maybe the kid went to live there with him."

"One thing about European movies," said Roy, "there's always more to think about afterwards than with American movies."

"Probably because they've got more history there," Frank said. "That's why more stuff happens in our movies. Americans don't like to think so much."

WAR IS MERELY ANOTHER KIND OF WRITING AND LANGUAGE

Walking into the A&P to buy a quart of milk, Roy spotted a tall, thin guy wearing an oversized hooded sweatshirt with the hood up and floppy pants watching a bunch of little kids playing in an empty lot. The guy had his back toward him but even though Roy could not see his face, Roy thought there was something peculiar about the way he was standing there, slightly slumped over, bent, not moving. The kids were very young, four, five and six years old, running and jumping around in the dirt and weeds. Roy was nine. He knew a few of the kids, one of whom was his friend Jimmy Boyle's younger brother, Paulie, who was six and a half.

Roy stopped and watched the guy frozen at the edge of the lot. It was a boiling hot day in July. The guy shouldn't be wearing a big sweatshirt with the hood up over his head, Roy thought. If he made a move toward the kids, Roy figured he could brain him with a rock. The empty lot was full of rocks and leftover half-bricks from when an addition to the Rogers house next door was built. Roy picked up a broken broom handle from the gutter in front of where he was standing. It had a sharp point on it.

The guy watched the kids for about two minutes more before he began shuffling away in the opposite direction from where Roy was headed. The kids probably had not even noticed him. When the guy turned the corner and was out of sight, Roy tossed the broom stick back into the gutter, then walked to the store.

When Roy came back carrying the milk, the kids were no longer in the empty lot. He walked to the corner the hooded guy had turned and Roy saw him about a quarter of the way down the block sitting at the edge of the sidewalk with his feet in the gutter. Roy still could not see his face. Nobody else was around. It was dinner time so the kids had gone to their houses. Roy stood looking at the curved figure on the sidewalk. He thought about going back for the broken broom handle, taking it and poking the guy and telling him to get up and keep moving. Just after he had this thought, the guy toppled forward and his entire body collapsed into the gutter.

A woman came out of a house next to where the guy was lying. She had a small dog on a leash, a black, brown and white mutt. The dog strained at the leash, trying to sniff the body, but the woman jerked him away. She walked the dog toward Roy.

"I saw that guy a little while ago watching some little kids playing in a vacant lot around the corner," Roy told her. "I thought he might be a child molester."

"It's Arthur Ray, Grace Lonergan's boy," said the woman. "He's not right in his head. I'll knock on her door and tell her to come and get him. He was hurt in Korea."

Roy knew there had been a war in Korea, which was a country near Japan and China, but he was not really sure where those countries were, only that they were very far from Chicago. Arthur Ray Lonergan probably had not known where or just how far away Korea was either until he went there.

THE END OF THE STORY

The dead man lying in the alley behind the Anderson house was identified by the police as James "Tornado" Thompson, a lone wolf stick-up man from Gary, Indiana. After robbing the currency exchange on Ojibway Boulevard in Chicago, he had gone out the front door holding a gun in one hand and was confronted on the sidewalk by two beat cops who were shooting the breeze before one of them went off duty. A clerk from the currency exchange appeared in the doorway and shouted, "Stop that man! He just robbed us!" Thompson pivoted and shot him. The cops pulled their guns but the thief dashed next door into the Green Harp Tavern and ran through the bar out the back door. One of the cops followed him; the other called for back up and for an ambulance to attend the wounded clerk, who was lying on the sidewalk.

Tornado Thompson ran down the alley. Roy and Jimmy Boyle and two of the McLaughlin brothers were playing ball when they saw Thompson speeding toward them holding a gun, followed by a cop.

"Holy shit!" yelled Jimmy Boyle. "Get down!"

The cop shouted, "Stop or I'll shoot!"

Thompson did not stop but stumbled over a crack in the uneven pavement and fell down, still gripping the gun. He twisted around and fired once at the cop, who stopped, dropped to one knee, aimed, and shot Tornado Thompson in the head.

"Stay down, boys!" said the cop.

He crept forward in a crouch, keeping his revolver trained on the robber. When he got to the body he determined the man was dead, then took the gun out of Thompson's hand and replaced his revolver in its holster.

Jimmy Boyle got up and rushed over to the body.

"Wow," he said, "you plugged him right in the forehead."

Roy and Johnny and Billy McLaughlin stood up and walked over. The cop stood up, too. A patrol car entered the alley from the Hammond Street end.

"Move away, boys," the cop said.

The car stopped and two cops got out. Another police car entered from the same direction and pulled up behind the first car. Two cops got out of it, too. They surrounded the body and the cop who'd shot Thompson told them what happened. A few neighbors, including Mr. Anderson, came out of the gangways of their houses. Three more police cars approached from the Ojibway Boulevard end of the alley. They stopped and six more cops joined the others.

"There ain't been so many people in the alley since Otto Polsky's garage burned down," said Johnny.

"He was refinishing a rowboat he'd built," Roy said, "and the shellac caught fire."

A few minutes later, an ambulance, its siren off, drove in off Hammond Street, stopped, and two men in white coats got out. One of them removed a stretcher from the rear of the ambulance, then they both walked over. After exchanging a few words with one of the cops, they lifted Thompson's body onto the stretcher, carried it to the ambulance, slid it in, and backed the ambulance out of the alley.

"What happened?" Mr. Anderson asked the boys.

"A guy come runnin' down the alley," said Jimmy, "with a cop chasin' him. The guy fired at the cop, the cop fired back and killed him."

"Hit him in the forehead," said Billy.

"Who was the guy?"

"I heard one of the cops say his name was Tornado Thompson, from Gary," Roy said. "He held up the currency exchange next to The Green Harp."

"He was a black guy," said Billy. "Why would he come all the way from Gary, Indiana, to Chicago to pull a hold up?"

The neighbors went back to their houses and all of the police cars left. Two cops remained in the alley, the cop who'd shot Tornado Thompson and the beat cop who'd stayed on Ojibway Boulevard.

"The detectives are at the currency exchange," said the beat cop.

"How's the clerk?"

"Dead."

"You fellas all right?" asked the cop who'd done the shooting.

The boys all nodded.

"Come on, Dom," said the other cop. "We got time to stop in the tavern, have a shot and a beer."

"Why was he called Tornado?" asked Roy.

"He was a halfback at the University of Indiana, eight, nine years ago," said Dom. "I saw him run back a kick-off ninety-four yards against Northwestern. It's how he got his nickname. I wish I hadn't had to shoot him."

The two cops walked up the alley. They boys watched them go through the back door of The Green Harp.

"I think I'd like to be a cop," said Billy.

The next afternoon, Roy's grandfather read to him from an article in the Chicago *Daily News* about the incident. The basic facts were there along with the additional information that a four year old Negro boy was found alone in a 1952 Plymouth parked a block away from the currency exchange. The boy was Tornado Thompson's son, Amos, who had been told by his father to wait in the car until he came back. A woman walking by had seen Amos Thompson sitting in the back seat of the Plymouth, crying. When she asked him what was wrong, the boy told her his father had been gone for a long time, that he didn't know where he was. The woman told a cop about the child in the car and he took Amos to the precinct station, where he informed the sergeant in charge that his mother and both of his grandmothers were dead and that he and his father had been living in their car because they didn't have any money. Amos was given over to The Simon the Cyrenian Refuge for Colored Children.

That's awful, Pops," said Roy.

"Yes, Roy, it is. And for Amos, it's not the end of the story."

INNOCENT OF THE BLOOD

From the first time he met him, Roy disliked Buddy Dobler. Dobler had an identical twin named Marty, so kids called them Buddy and Marty Double. It was easy to tell them apart because Buddy was taller and heavier and was more assertive than his brother. Marty was quiet and good-natured, whereas Buddy was abrasive and mean-spirited. The twins attended a different grammar school than Roy, but they lived not too far away from Roy's neighborhood, and hung out with his friends Johnny Murphy and Tommy Cunningham, whose families were members of the same church as the Doblers.

Buddy and Marty were in the eighth grade and Roy was in the seventh, as were Johnny and Tommy.

"Buddy beat up a grown man by himself," Johnny Murphy told Roy. "Tommy saw him do it."

Johnny and Roy were walking on Ojibway Avenue going to meet Tommy and the Doblers at Blood of Our Savior Park. It was the first day of December but no snow had fallen yet in Chicago. The temperature was just above freezing and wind was gusting hard off the lake. Both boys were wearing leather jackets, earmuffs and gloves.

"Who'd he beat up?"

"A wino on Clark Street was bummin' for change. Tommy said Double clobbered the guy with a garbage can lid."

"Was the guy big?"

"Tommy didn't say. He was just a regular-sized wino."

"I don't like him."

"Who? Buddy Dobler?"

"Yeah. I think he's a jerk. He likes to push people around."

"He do somethin' to you?"

"I don't hardly know him. His brother's okay, though."

"Their mother was in a mental hospital."

"How do you know?"

"I heard my parents talkin' about it. My dad said Mrs. Dobler cut her wrists and her throat and almost died."

"When was this?"

"She got out of the bin two or three months ago. Maybe Buddy's angry about his mother so he takes it out on other people."

At Blood of Our Savior the Dobler twins were kneeling on the ground next to the basketball court shooting craps with Tommy Cunningham and another kid Roy didn't recognize.

"Who's that?" Roy asked Johnny. "The guy with the right side of his head shaved."

"Harley Fox. He's fourteen or fifteen. Remember him? He got sent to St. Charles after he set his five year old cousin on fire. They kept him in a year. He goes to a special school now."

Buddy Dobler was holding the dice. Coins and a few dollar bills were on the ground. Buddy kissed the dice, said, "Come on, eight," and threw them.

One die rolled off the concrete into the dirt. It turned up three. The other die showed four.

"You lose," said Harley Fox.

"It don't count," said Buddy, and scooped up both dice. "One of 'em fell off."

"The hell it don't," said Harley. He picked up the money. "Pass the dice."

Buddy Dobler chucked the dice hard at Fox's face and jumped on him. Both Tommy and Marty Dobler stood up quickly, got out of the way, and watched Buddy and Harley wrestle, as did Roy and Johnny Murphy.

Buddy got to his feet, grabbed hold of Harley's left leg and dragged him around in the dirt. Fox was on his back and Roy could see that on the shaved side of his head were several stitches. Fox was trying to twist away but he couldn't until Buddy tripped backwards over the low curb bordering a footpath. Harley Fox sprang to his feet and kicked Buddy in the head. He was wearing motorcycle boots and Dobler stayed down. Fox kicked him a few more times and then stomped down as hard as he could with the heel of his left boot on Buddy's face.

Harley was shorter than Buddy but he outweighed him by twenty pounds. Dobler wasn't moving or saying anything. Blood ran out of his nose and the sides of his mouth and his eyes were closed. Fox took a book of matches out of the right pocket of his bomber jacket, struck one, lit the matchbook, bent down and set fire to Buddy's hair. Marty took off his coat and tried to smother the flames but Harley stopped him, wrenched the coat out of Marty's hands and tossed it aside.

"The old lady nurses at St. Charles are tougher than your brother," Harley Fox said to him.

Fox turned and walked away. The back of his head and jacket were covered with mud. Marty picked up his coat and went to cover his brother's hair, but the fire was already out. Buddy's forehead was singed and the front of his hair had been burned off. He still was not moving.

"We gotta call an ambulance," said Tommy.

Johnny Murphy picked a dime out of the dirt and said, "There's a pay phone in the drugstore next to the park. I'll go call."

Marty Dobler was sitting on the ground, staring at Buddy. Tommy came over and stood by Roy.

"I guess Fox learned how to fight like that in the reformatory," he said.

"Setting someone on fire is his own idea," said Roy.

Johnny Murphy came back and said, "I told the drugstore owner what happened, so he called."

When the emergency medical crew lifted Buddy onto a stretcher, he groaned a little, but he did not move or open his eyes. Marty went along with him in the ambulance.

"I should go tell Buddy's parents so they can meet him at the hospital," said Tommy.

"Here's the dime I was gonna use," Johnny said, digging it out of his right front pants pocket and handing it to him. "Talk to Mr. Dobler. You know his wife's not right in the head."

"What do you think'll happen to Harley?" asked Tommy.

"Buddy started the fight," said Roy.

"True," said Tommy, "but Harley torched him. Walk over to the drugstore with me. After I make the call we can get somethin' to eat."

As they passed the sign Blood of Our Savior Park, Roy thought about why he did not feel bad or upset about Buddy Dobler being hurt; he wondered if he should, even though he didn't like him. When Tommy went into the drugstore, Johnny and Roy waited outside.

"I guess Buddy deserved a beatin'," Johnny said. "None of us jumped in to help him until Marty tried to put out the fire on his head. Maybe Buddy is a jerk, like you said."

"When Jesus was carrying the cross," said Roy, "nobody jumped in to help him, either."

THE ITALIAN HAT

Roy's mother's friend June DeLisa was the kind of woman who would fly from Chicago to Venice, Italy, just to buy a hat. She did this in September of 1956, and when she returned Roy's mother asked her what was so special about the hat.

"It's handmade, of course, and designed by a man named Tito Verdi, who claims to be related to the famous composer. He's very old, in his late eighties or early nineties. The materials he uses are woven by crones in the hills of Puglia. Anyway, how do you like it?"

The hat perched perilously on the right side of June DeLisa's head. Other than an extraordinarily brilliant yellow-green feather attached to the radically raked left side of the tri-corner, Kitty thought the hat unremarkable; even the crumpled blue material that formed the construction looked like it could have been purchased for a dollar ninety-eight at Woolworth's.

"I like the feather. I've never seen such a radiant yellow before."

"Plucked from a rare species in the Belgian Congo."

"Dare I ask what you paid for it?"

"You daren't."

June DeLisa's husband had made a fortune on the commodities market. Kitty and June had met before either of them had gotten married, when they both modelled fur coats at the Merchandise Mart.

"How was Venice?"

"It's always lovely at this time of year, unless there's a hot spell. You've never been, have you? Crowded, but still like being in a dream, especially just after dawn."

"Did Lloyd go with you?"

"Oh, no. He has his polo to occupy him. And Mrs. Gringold."

"I thought he'd ended it with her."

Roy came into the livingroom, where his mother and June DeLisa were seated on the sofa.

"Goodness, Roy," June said, "you're growing up so fast. How old are you now?"

"I'll be eight next month."

"Mrs. DeLisa has just returned from Italy. She's telling me about her trip."

"Do you like my new hat, Roy? I had it made for me over there."

"It looks like the one Robin Hood wears, only his is brown, not blue."

"What is it, sweetheart? I thought you were going to play outside with the Murphy boys."

"It's raining, so I'm going to build a model in my room."

"Let me know if you need anything. If June and I decide to go out, I'll tell you."

Roy left the room. He did not dislike June DeLisa, but seeing her made him think that she was going to go home and jump out a window from her apartment on the 30th floor of the building she lived in on Lake Shore Drive.

"So he's seeing Anastasia again."

"He never really stopped. I'll probably have to kill her, or get a divorce. If I decide to have her killed, would you mind if I asked Rudy about getting someone to do it? You and he are still on good terms, aren't you?"

"Stop it, June. Don't even talk like that. Of course Rudy and I are on good terms. We're very close, and he sees Roy once or twice a week. Rudy loves his son more than anything."

"What about your mother?"

"She's too sick now to do anything about it."

"As if she hasn't already done enough."

"Since I divorced Rudy, she's actually begun to be more respectful of him."

"Rose respects what he can do, or have done, you mean."

"He provides very well for Roy."

"And for you, too, I hope."

"I can't complain."

"He still loves you, Kitty. He always will. You're luckier for that. Lloyd never cared for me the way Rudy does you."

"He doesn't love Anastasia, I don't think. Does she love Lloyd?"

"If Maurice Gringold didn't own two banks and half the state of Ohio, I doubt she would stay married to him."

"Take off that hat, June. Just looking at it makes me nervous."

June removed her hat and put it down on the coffee table.

"I feel useless, Kitty. If Lloyd and I had children I don't suppose I would."

Rain was coming down hard. The two women sat without talking and listened to it bang against the windows and the roof.

"I asked old Signore Verdi how he had come to be a hat maker and he told me it was because he was a lousy violinist. Isn't that funny?"

Kitty looked at June's hat.

"Did Verdi tell you that feather came from the Belgian Congo?"

THE SENEGALESE TWIST

Roy had walked for several blocks before he realized he was lost. His friend Danny Luna had moved with his family to a new neighborhood and Roy was looking for their house. Danny had told him it was on the edge of Chinatown on Rhinelander Avenue, an apartment above the Far East Laundromat, a few blocks south of Superior. Danny's father worked as a drover in the Stockyards pens and his mother, a seamstress, was from Tell City, Indiana, a Swiss community. Danny said she had run away from Tell City when she was sixteen and come to Chicago, where she met his father, an illegal immigrant from Juarez, Mexico.

Since Danny was born, the Luna family had moved twelve times, one for each year of his life. He and Roy had played together on baseball teams for the past two years and Roy wanted to get him to play second base on the Tecumseh Cubs, for whom Roy was going to be the shortstop. The Lunas did not have a telephone, otherwise Roy would have called him.

Roy found himself on the corner of Menominee and Van Buren streets. He had no idea where Rhinelander Avenue was, so he decided to ask someone. He went into a beauty shop called Miss Racy's Powder Room, figuring there had to be a woman in there who could give him directions. Roy was surprised to see that all of the women in Miss Racy's Powder Room, both the customers and hair stylists, were black.

A slender girl with skin the color of maple syrup came up to

Roy and said, loud enough for everyone to hear, "Don't tell me you're lookin' for your mama, baby, 'cause she ain't been here."

All of the women laughed, and the girl, who looked to Roy to be about eighteen, poked Roy on his chest with the long, purple painted nails on the two middle fingers of her right hand. She had red hair that stood up at least eight inches from her head, brown eyes with blue shadow on the lids, and freckles all over her face.

"What's your problem, sweetness?" she asked.

"I'm looking for Rhinelander Avenue. A friend of mine lives there over the Far East Laundromat."

"What your friend can do for you I can't?"

Most of the women were no longer paying attention to Roy and the girl, but the few who were giggled and shouted, "Rock that cradle, Red!", "His mama do find her way here, she gonna close us down!" and "Quit scarin' that boy, Charleen. He ain't big enough to do you right no how!"

"How old are you, sugar?" the girl asked Roy.

"Twelve and a half."

"That's what my milkman delivers every Tuesday and Friday," said a woman with a scalpful of green paste, which made one woman howl and say, "Uh huh."

Roy looked around the walls, which were decorated with posters from the Regal Theater and Aragon Ballroom featuring photographs of Ruth Brown, Chuck Jackson, Sarah Vaughan and Nat "King" Cole. Also tacked up were signs advertising hair straightening, skin lightening, manicures and pedicures. But the one that intrigued Roy read, "We Do Senegalese Twist".

"You got good, wavy hair," the girl said. "Be longer than most boys."

"I don't like getting haircuts," said Roy.

She ran her painted fingers through his hair from back to front, then front to back.

"I could do somethin' nice with it."

"What's the Senegalese Twist? It sounds like a kind of dance."

"Show it to him, Charleen," crowed Green Paste, "out back!"

"It's okay," said Roy, "I'll find Rhinelander. Thanks, anyway."

He opened the door to the street and went out. Before he could walk away, one of Charleen's hands was on his left shoulder. Roy turned around and looked at her.

"We call it Chopsticks Street," she said. "Go up a block on Van Buren, then right until you run into it. What's your name?"

"Roy."

"Mine is Charleen. C-h-a-r-l-e-e-n. You tall for your age, Roy. Almost tall as me, and I'm seventeen. I be in Miss Racy's every day but Sunday and Monday you want to take me up on my offer."

"I live pretty far away from here."

Charleen's freckles glittered in the sunlight. A butterfly landed on top of her high-piled hair.

"There's a butterfly on your head."

"Those ladies, they get raunchy, don't they? Miss Racy say the reason I'm attracted to very young boys is because my stepdaddy messed with me. He's gone now. Marleen, my sister, she cut off his privates while he was sleepin' and he bled to death. He was messin' with her, too. The butterfly still there?"

"Yes."

"He like me. You like me you know me better."

She tilted her head and the butterfly flitted off.

"Thanks, Charleen. I've got to go."

Later, Roy asked Danny Luna how he liked living in the neighborhood, and Danny said, "I don't know anybody yet except for the Chinese kids downstairs."

"I know where your mother can get her hair done," said Roy.

KIDNAPPED

Foster Wildroot disappeared on a Tuesday morning in early November of 1956. He was last seen on his way to school, walking on Minnetonka Street at a quarter to nine as he did every weekday morning. Foster's mother told police on Wednesday that before he left the house her son, who was ten years old and in the fourth grade, had eaten a piece of rye toast with strawberry jam on it, drunk half a cup of black coffee and taken with him an apple to eat at recess. The weather was unusually warm for November, so Foster wore only a blue peacoat, which he did not button up, and did not take either a hat or gloves. He was small for his age, said Frieda Wildroot, and very shy. Foster did not have many friends, almost none, really, she told them; he kept mostly to himself. He had brown hair, cut short, and wore black-framed glasses to correct his severe near-sightedness. Foster stuttered badly, she said, an impediment that hampered his ability to orally answer questions put to him in the classroom. As a result, Foster disliked school. She did not, however, believe he would run away from home, as that was his sanctuary, where he spent his time alone in his room building model airplanes.

Foster's father, Fred Wildroot, did not live in Chicago with his wife and son. At present, Frieda told the authorities, her husband was working in a coal mine in West Virginia, from where he mailed her a support check every month. The police asked if she thought it was possible that Foster would try to go to West Virginia to see his father, and she said that Fred Wildroot had neither seen nor communicated with his son since the boy was six years old.

"Fred moves around a lot," said Frieda. "Foster wouldn't even know where to go to find him."

Foster Wildroot was in Roy's class but since he did not talk much or participate in sports on the playground, which was Roy's main interest, they did not really know each other. None of Roy's friends knew much about Wildroot; like Roy, they saw him only in school, where he sat by choice in the last seat of the back row in the classroom. Foster had been absent from school for a week or more before Roy noticed he was not there. Even after he did, Roy figured the kid was sick or that his family had moved away. Many people left Chicago during the 1950s, most of them relocating to the West Coast, primarily to Los Angeles.

"Wildroot lives on your block, doesn't he?" Roy asked Billy Katz. "What do you think happened to him?"

"My mother thinks he was kidnapped by a pervert," said Katz. "She says Chicago's full of perverts. Wildroot's probably locked in a basement where the perv feeds him steaks and ice cream to keep him happy after he does shit to him."

"I just hope they don't find his body dumped in the forest preserves with his head cut off, like those sisters," Roy said. "They were our age, too."

"He stayed inside his house all the time," said Billy. "I hardly seen him. He didn't play with any of the other kids on the block, neither. My mother says his mother works part-time ironing sheets and stuff at the Disciples of Festus House for the Pitiful on Washtenaw, but I don't know how she knows."

"What about his father?"

"Never around. Maybe he don't have one."

Foster Wildroot was never seen again, at least not in Roy's neighborhood. Billy Katz said Mrs. Wildroot still lived in the same house, though, and one day, about six months after Foster went missing, Mr. Wildroot showed up.

"My mother seen him," said Billy. "Tall, skinny guy, walked with a cane."

"How'd your mother know it was Foster's father?"

"He went to every house on the block and handed a card to whoever answered the door, or else he put one in the mailbox if nobody was home, then he went away. My mother said he didn't talk to anyone."

"What does it say on the cards?"

"If anyone knows what happened to my son, Foster Wildroot, please write to Mr. Fred Wildroot at a post office box in Montana or Utah, someplace like that."

A year later, Roy and Billy Katz were playing catch with a football in the alley behind Billy's house when Billy pointed to a woman dumping the contents of a large, cardboard box into a garbage can behind a garage a few houses away.

"That's Mrs. Wildroot," he told Roy.

After the woman went back into her house, Billy said, "Let's go see what she put in there."

The garbage can was full of model airplanes, most of them missing wings or with broken propellers.

"See any you want to take?" asked Billy.

THE DOLPHINS

Roy's Uncle Buck built a house on Utila, one of the Bay Islands of Honduras. It was an octagonal structure with eight doors on a spit of land accessible only by boat when the tide was in. Buck had transported a generator, refrigerator and other appliances on the ship *Islander Trader* from St. Petersburg, Florida, to Utila, and when he returned on the same boat two and a half months later, Roy met him at the dock.

"I had to go to Teguci for a few days to renew my residency visa and take care of some other business," Buck told him, "and I was walking down a street with my friend Goodnight Morgan, who used to live on Utila but now lives on Roatan, when a car came by, slowed down, and someone fired three shots at us, then sped away. Neither of us were hit. Drive-bys are common in Tegucigalpa, it's the murder capital of Latin America, if not the world, but I didn't know why anyone would want to kill us. Goodnight Morgan used to be High Sheriff of Utila, so I asked him if he thought he could have been targeted by a political rival or a criminal who held a grudge against him. Goodnight said either was possible, but he didn't think so. 'Gangsters in Teguci kill for no reason other than to intimidate the population,' he said. 'That's why almost nobody is on the streets. To shop they go to malls where there are security guards with automatic weapons to protect them.'"

Roy and his uncle were driving on the bridge over the bay on their way to Tampa when Buck said, "The *Islander Trader* started leaking fuel when we were a day from port, and the radio was on the fritz. We barely made it to Roatan. The leak had to be patched up before going on to Utila. Then came the shooting in Teguci. Keep in mind, nephew, when a person walks out the door you might never see him or her again."

It was a hot and humid day, which was not unusual, but the exceptionally heavy cloud cover, without wind, portended rain, at the very least.

"This weather reminds me of the time I was in Callao, waiting for a ship to take me to Panama City, where I could get a plane to Miami," said Buck. "Hundreds of dolphins invaded the harbor, making it impossible for boats to get in or out. They sensed that a giant storm was coming and they were trying to get out of its way. I'll never forget the sight of those blue-green dolphins crowded together like cattle in the stockyards in Chicago. Dolphins are big, the adults average seven feet long, and they were jabbering to each other, loud, squealing and honking that drowned out everything else."

"Did a big storm hit?"

"About four hours later, the rain started, then huge waves inundated the Peruvian coast, followed by a hailstorm, the kind you get in Kansas or Oklahoma. Nobody there had even seen hail before. All of the ships tied up or at anchor in and near the harbor were damaged, and a number of boats out at sea capsized."

"What about the dolphins?"

"They dove deeper to avoid the hail. But when the bad weather passed, the dolphins were all gone, no sight or sound of them. They were already miles away in the Pacific."

"How long were you stuck in Callao?"

"About a week. I went to Lima for a couple of days, then went back to get my ship."

Rain hit the windshield, so Roy slowed the car down. They were almost across the bridge.

"Dolphins are smart, Roy, they know when and how to escape from the weather and other cetaceans. Human beings are the biggest threat to their existence. I told Goodnight Morgan about the dolphins in Callao, and you know what he said?"

Roy shook his head.

"That's why you never see any dolphins walking down the street in Tegucigalpa."

DRAGONLAND

Roy's mother was having trouble sleeping. When she mentioned this to her friend Kay, she recommended that Kitty make an appointment to see Dr. Flynn.

"Is he a sleep expert?" Kitty asked.

"He has a medical degree in orthopedics," said Kay, "but he specializes in hypnotherapy now."

"I don't want to be hypnotized. I just need a scrip for sleeping pills until I'm myself again."

"Better to see Flynn than take pills. You'll get strung out on them and have a bigger problem. Dr. Flynn is kind of a genius. He uses hypnotism to correct bodily deformities based on his theory that malformations of the body are caused by psychological conditions."

"You mean he cures cripples by hypnosis?"

"I know it sounds daffy, but apparently he's had great success."

"Where did he go to medical school, in Tibet?"

"Go see him, Kitty. Try it once, then tell me if you think he's a quack. And even if he is, if what he does cures your insomnia what difference will it make?"

The day after Roy's mother saw Dr. Flynn she called Kay to give her the report.

"He's a nice man with good manners. Dyes his hair. We talked for a while, and he asked me if anything in particular had been bothering me lately. I told him I've had trouble sleeping periodically since I was a child. Now, since my divorce, I've been having difficulty again, and that when I do fall asleep I often have bad dreams."

"Did he hypnotize you?"

"I suppose so."

"What do you mean 'suppose'? Did he or didn't he?"

"He said he did. He didn't swing a watch or anything in front of my eyes. He just spoke to me and then I felt a little dizzy. I guess I passed out for a few minutes. Afterwards I felt relaxed. That's all."

"Did you sleep better last night?"

"Roy had to wake me up this morning to get his breakfast. I'm always up before he is."

"How did you feel?"

"Like I didn't get enough sleep. Not exhausted but vague. I think yesterday tired me out."

"What did Flynn say? Are you going to see him again?"

"I don't know, Kay. He left it up to me. I had a strange dream last night."

"Do you remember it?"

"I was walking alone on a city street in the middle of the night. I had no destination, I was just walking. There were other women like me, walking, because they were crazy and couldn't stop. I was afraid and some of them laughed at me. One of the women said, 'Welcome to Dragonland.' I wanted to go home but I was lost and only these crazy women were there."

"Did you ever have this dream before?"

"It wasn't only a dream, Kay. I did this for real lots of times. I never told anyone."

"Rudy didn't know?"

"It happened once when he and I were first together. I told him I was restless and needed to get some fresh air. We were in a hotel room, three o'clock in the morning. I told him not to worry, to go back to sleep, and I went out."

"What about Dr. Flynn? Did you tell him?"

"Maybe, when I was hypnotized."

"What about Roy?"

"What about him?"

"Do you want him to stay with me and Marvin for a couple of days? Until you're feeling better."

"I feel all right. Thanks for offering. Roy's no trouble."

That night Kitty couldn't sleep. She had an urge to leave the house, to walk, but she was afraid to leave Roy alone. She looked at herself in the bedroom mirror and thought about what Dr. Flynn had told her before she left his office.

"There's nothing terribly wrong with you," he said, "Go back to work."

"I used to be a model," she told him.

Kitty went into the livingroom and turned on the TV. Ava Gardner was dancing barefoot in the rain. She didn't look happy, either.

ROLE MODEL

On Roy's fourteenth birthday he came home from school and found his mother sitting alone at the kitchen table drinking a cup of coffee and reading *Holiday* magazine.

"Hi, Ma," he said. "What are you reading?"

"An article about Brazil. You know I was there once."

"You told me. Who were you there with?"

"Oh, a boyfriend. It was before I met your father. We spent a week in Rio. The beaches were lovely, the sand was so white, but very crowded, as crowded as Times Square on New Year's Eve. The Carioca girls were almost naked, brown and slithery and beautiful. I had a wonderful time."

"Why haven't you ever gone back?"

"Rio's not the kind of place your father would have liked, and since he died I've not had the opportunity."

It was a dreary day, drizzly and gray and colder than usual for the time of year. Roy knew his mother preferred warm weather.

"It's my birthday today."

"I know, Roy. Are you going out with your friends?"

"Later, maybe. Right now I'm going to work. I just came home to change my clothes."

"Your father always dressed well. People used to dress better in the old days."

"You mean in the 1940s?"

"Yes. Before then, too."

"Well, I'm going to be boiling hot dogs and frying hamburgers. It wouldn't be a good idea for me to wear a suit."

"No, Roy, of course not. That's not what I mean. It's just that people cared more for their appearance when I was young."

"This is 1961, Ma, and you're only thirty-four. You're still young."

Roy was standing next to the table. His mother looked up at him and smiled. She really is still beautiful, he thought. She had long auburn hair, dark brown eyes, perfect teeth and very red lips.

"I know you miss your father, Roy. It's a shame he died so young."

"He was a strong person," Roy said. "People liked and respected him, didn't they?"

"Yes. He handled things his own way. People trusted him. You know your father never gave me more than twenty-five dollars a week spending money, but I could go into any department store or good restaurant and charge whatever I wanted. I'll tell you something that happened not long after he and I were married. We were living in the Seneca Hotel, where you were born, and there was another couple in the hotel we were friends with, Ricky and Rosita Danillo. Rosita was a little older than I—she was from Puerto Rico—and Ricky was a few years younger than your dad, who was nineteen years older than me."

"What business was Ricky in?"

"Oh, the rackets, like everybody in Chicago, but he wasn't in your father's league. He looked up to Rudy. Anyway, late one afternoon your father came home and I was wearing a new hat, blood red with a veil, and he said it looked good on me. I told him I was just trying it on. He asked me where I'd gotten it and I said it was a gift from Ricky Danillo, that I'd come back to the hotel

244

after having lunch with Peggy Spain and the concierge handed me a hatbox with a note from Ricky."

"What did the note say?"

"I don't remember exactly, something about how he hoped I'd like it, that when he saw it in a shop window he thought it suited my style. Your dad didn't say anything but the next day when I went down to the lobby I saw that one of the plate glass windows in the front was boarded up. I asked the concierge what happened and he told me that Rudy had punched Ricky Danillo and knocked him through the window, then told the hotel manager to put the cost of replacing it on his bill. That night I said to your dad, 'You knocked Ricky through a plate glass window just because he bought me a hat?'"

"What did he say?"

"'No, Kitty, I did it because he didn't ask me first.' That's the kind of guy your father was. I didn't say another word about it."

"What happened to the hat?"

"I never wore it. I gave it away to someone."

Roy did not tell anyone at work that it was his birthday and afterwards he was too tired to go anywhere. When he got home there was a chocolate cake on the kitchen table with fifteen yellow candles stuck in it. His mother wasn't home. He picked up a book of matches that was on the stove and lit the candles, then took off his wet jacket and draped it over the back of a chair. Roy thought about making a wish but he couldn't think of one. He blew out the candles anyway.

MONA

"What's goin' on?"

"Two guys held up the Black Hawk Savings and Loan. A teller set off the alarm and the cops showed up just as the robbers were comin' out. They shot the first one out the door, he's dead, but the other one ran across the street into the Uptown. He's holed up in there."

"What's playin'?"

"*Tell Him I'm Dangerous.* You seen it?"

"No. How long's he been in the theater?"

"Twenty minutes, half hour. The cops got the exits covered. They don't want a shootout inside, innocent people get hurt."

Roy had been on his way home from Minnetonka Park when he saw a crowd on the sidewalk on Broadway. He spotted Bobby Dorp right away because Dorp was six foot six and towered over everybody. Bobby was a junior in high school, two years ahead of Roy, who knew him from pick-up basketball games.

"I was goin' into Lingenberg's to get a cake for my mother when I heard the shots," said Dorp. "I come over here and saw a body lyin' in front of the bank with blood pourin' out of it. He musta been drilled twenty times. The other robber was already in the theater. He might be wounded."

"It's a matinee, so there probably aren't too many people in there," said Roy. "It'll be dark in less than an hour. I think the cops'll wait him out."

By now the street was clogged with police cars and patrolmen had the theater surrounded.

Dorp said, "I gotta get my mother's cake before Lingenberg's closes. Don't let the shootin' start until I get back."

Marksmen with high-powered rifles were positioning themselves on the roofs of buildings around the Uptown. The only way the robber could escape, Roy figured, was to pretend he was a patron. To do that, the guy would have to ditch his weapon and the bank money, if he had any. Hiding a bullet wound might be tough, though, depending on where he'd been hit.

As darkness fell, spotlights were set up on nearby rooftops. No traffic was moving in the immediate vicinity. Bobby Dorp came back carrying a cake box.

"I got there just in time," he said, "or they woulda sold this cake, too. Lingenberg's is sellin' out the place. Seein' men die makes people hungry, I guess. I never seen it so crowded."

"I wonder if they're sellin' popcorn and candy in the Uptown," said Roy.

A middleaged woman in front of the boys fainted and fell off the curb. Two men helped her to her feet and led her away. The sun was gone.

"I can't stay no longer," said Dorp. "Gotta get the cake home. Anyway, it's gettin' cold. Maybe I'll come back after dinner."

After Bobby Dorp left, Roy moved closer to the front, so that he had an unobstructed view of the theater entrance. Sawhorses had been lined up along the curb. Every cop in sight had his gun drawn.

Men and women began walking out of the theater with their hands held above their heads. Some of them were crying. Police took each person into custody as soon as they reached the sidewalk. Thirty or forty people came out and were loaded into paddy wagons. The cops kept their guns trained on the entrance.

"He's still inside," a man said.

"Go in and get him!" yelled another man.

"There he is!" screamed a woman, pointing at the roof of the theater.

Everyone looked up. A man was standing near the edge of the roof, directly over the marquee. He was bareheaded and was wearing a brown hunter's vest over a red and black checkered shirt and dark green trousers. He looked to be about twenty-five or thirty years old.

"Put your hands on your head!" a policeman ordered through a bullhorn.

The man did not comply. He just stood there with his hands by his sides.

"Place your hands over your head or you will be shot!" warned the cop with the horn.

The man said something but Roy could not make out the words.

"What did he say?" asked the woman who'd spotted him on the roof.

The man spoke again and this time Roy heard him say "Mona."

"Mona?" the woman said. "Did he say Mona?"

The riflemen fired, hitting him from sixteen directions. The man fell forward into the well of the marquee. A dozen pigeons fluttered out. All Roy could see now was the theater sign, black letters on a white background: TELL HIM I'M DANGEROUS PLUS CARTOONS.

Roy elbowed his way out of the crowd and started walking. All that was missing, he thought, was snow falling on the thief's lifeless body. Lingenberg's Bakery was still open. Roy went inside.

"Do you have any doughnuts left?" he asked a pink-faced, blonde woman behind the counter.

"Yust one," she said. "Chocolate."

"I'll take it."

"I hear many noises together. Something happen?"

"The police shot and killed a man."

Roy gave the woman a dime. She took it and handed him the doughnut wrapped in wax paper.

"What reason for?" she asked.

Roy took a bite, chewed and swallowed it.

"Mona," he said.

MUD

When Leni Haakonen was eight and nine years old she liked playing war or cowboys and Indians with Roy, who was the same age. She was a Swedish girl who lived with her mother in a tenement apartment on the corner of the block, two buildings down from where Roy lived with his mother. Her father had been killed in the war and Roy's parents were divorced. There was a vacant lot next to the building Leni lived in where she and Roy often played. Leni was as tough as any boy Roy knew, including himself, and she was very pretty. Most of the time she wore her honey-brown hair in two long braids; she had gray-blue eyes and a small red birthmark on her left cheek, and for as long as Roy knew her Leni never wore a dress.

One afternoon in late August they were pretending to be soldiers, rolling in the dirt and weeds of the vacant lot, when Leni asked Roy to kiss her. She was lying on her back and her face was dusty and smudged.

"I'm going to be nine tomorrow," Leni said to Roy, "and I've never kissed a boy. I want you to be the first."

Roy had kissed girls before but he had not thought even once about kissing Leni. He hesitated and looked at her. She had a fierce expression on her face, the same as when the two of them wrestled.

"Kiss me, Roy. On the lips."

There was mud on her mouth. Roy wiped it off with his right thumb and kissed her. Both of them kept their eyes open.

"My mother wanted me to only invite girls to my birthday party," she said. "That's why you didn't get an invitation."

The kiss had lasted two seconds. Leni rolled away from Roy and stood up. He stood up, too.

"Which girls did you invite?"

"None. It's just going to be me and my mother and her sister, my Aunt Terry, and her daughter, my cousin Lucy. Lucy's twelve. I don't like her but my mother says she has to come because of Aunt Terry. I don't like her, either. I'm getting a new winter coat, a white one with a red collar. I can save a piece of cake and give it to you the day after tomorrow. It'll be a yellow cake with chocolate frosting."

Leni and her mother moved away before she and Roy were ten. Seventeen years later, a few months after Roy's first novel was published, he received the following letter in care of his publisher in New York. The name on the return address on the envelope was Mrs. Robert Mitchell.

Dear Roy, I hope you remember me. We used to play together when we were children and I lived in Chicago. My mother and I moved to Grand Rapids, Michigan, when I was ten, or almost. Now I live in Detroit with my husband who is a dentist. I work as a receptionist in his office.

I bought your book and wanted to tell you. I have not read all of it because there are too many parts I do not really understand but I like the photograph of you on the back cover. You look like I thought you would.

Robert and I do not have children. I don't want any

but he does. My mother lives in Grand Rapids with her sister.

I probably should not tell you this in writing but I want to. Sometimes I can still feel your thumb on my lips when you wiped off the mud that time. It was on the day before my ninth birthday. I don't expect you to remember.

If you ever come to Detroit look me up. On the book it says that you live in Paris, France, so I don't really think I'll see you here or ever. You probably get other letters like this.

Sincerely,

Leni (Haakonen) Mitchell

THE PHANTOM FATHER

Roy's father was born on August 13, 1910, in the village of Siret, in what following World War II became Romania, close to the border of Ukraine. Soon thereafter, he moved with his family to Vienna, the capital city of the Austro-Hungarian empire. They were Austrian citizens. In 1917, the family resided at number five Zirkusgasse in the neighborhood of Leopoldstadt, near the ferris wheel in Luna Park Roy would first glimpse in director Carol Reed's film *The Third Man*. Roy's grandfather's profession as listed in the Vienna city directory of that year was printer. The Great War ended in December of 1918, at which point the family—father, two sons, one daughter, mother—made their way to Czernowitz, where they remained until April 1921, when they left for Antwerp, Belgium, from which port they took ship on the 14th of that month aboard the S.S. *Finland* bound for New York. From New York City they continued to Chicago, Illinois, where the family established residence for the remainder of their lives. They were Jews, fortunate to escape Europe before the Nazis perpetrated their murderous campaign to expunge the race from the continent.

Roy's father, who died at the age of forty-eight on December 5, 1958, not quite two months after Roy's twelfth birthday, never spoke to him of his Austrian childhood, nor did Roy ever hear him speak either German or Yiddish, as his father did. (Roy's grandmother died before he was born.) He became an American, a Chicagoan, and a criminal who was arrested several times for receiving stolen property and violations of the Volstead Act, known as Prohibition, during the years when the sale of liquor was illegal in the United States. His longest jail term was one year. Roy was, therefore, by birth a first-generation American, the son of a gangster who died young. Like his father, Roy eventually made his own way without much help. He wanted to know where his father came from, so he travelled first to Vienna, later to Romania, and found out. What Roy discovered did not surprise him; what did surprise him was that among those who had been closest to him, Roy was alone in his interest: neither his brother nor his mother particularly cared. Roy was not sure why he thought they would.

For Roy, the question that remained was why, during the twelve years he knew him, his father chose never to share with him any information, let alone details, of his or his immediate family's pre-American existence. As William Faulkner famously stated, "The past is not dead, it's not even past." This was a sentiment with which Roy agreed, and so he hated knowing that he would never know.

For his seventh birthday, in 1953, on an unseasonably cold and snowy October afternoon in Chicago, Roy's mother took him and a few of his friends to see the movie *Phantom from Space*. It was in black and white and the title figure could appear and disappear at will; one moment visible to earthlings, invisible the next. This is how Roy's father remained in his memory, a kind of phantom, there but not there, and no longer here; not enough for Roy.

ROY'S LETTER

Dear Dad,

It's almost Christmas of 1962. You died four years ago, when I was twelve. We didn't talk after you went into the hospital for the last time. Mom told me to call you there and I tried the night before you died but the nurse said you couldn't talk. The next day Mom asked me why I hadn't called you and I told her I did but she didn't believe me. I don't know why. She was acting crazy maybe because you were dead saying she was going to faint. She went out on a date that night and didn't tell me you might die. She's talking about getting married again which would make this her fourth marriage since you and she were divorced. I was five then and didn't really understand what that meant. By the time I was eleven I understood that it was up to me to take care of myself. You had a new wife and the man my mother was married to and I did not like each other. Anyway, he didn't last much longer with her. You remember I got a job delivering Chinese food on a bicycle for 25 cents an hour and a dime a delivery plus tips. I've been working ever since, mostly in hot dog and hamburger places. I give Mom money every month for her and my sister, who was born a few months after you died. Mom is working part time as a receptionist in a private hospital. I hope she doesn't get married again until after I graduate from high school. I'll be gone then and not have to deal with another guy who doesn't want me around.

I'm not sure what I want to be yet but I write stories and articles about sports. I'm a pretty good athlete, especially in baseball. I remember all of the times we spent together in Chicago and Key West and Miami and Havana. I wish we could still go to Cuba. I miss the people and the food there. I remember one morning when we were having breakfast on the terrace at the Nacional and there were some very beautiful girls sitting near us and you told me Cuban women didn't usually have big breasts but their rear ends were exceptional. I liked the weather there even though it got so hot. I won't live in Chicago after I finish high school. I don't know if I'll go to college even though Uncle Buck says I should. He wants me to be a civil engineer like him, or an architect, but I don't think I will. I just want to go places, to travel everywhere that interests me and see what happens and write about it. You were only a few years younger than I am now when you came to America from the old country. Other than wishing you were still alive I wish I could have known you when you were a boy, that both of us could have been boys at the same time and that we could have been friends.

Love, your son,

Roy